To Sol & Patty
Best,
John Crow
(Dennis Lynds)

WHEN THEY KILL YOUR WIFE

WHEN THEY KILL YOUR WIFE

YOUR WIFE

JOHN CROWE
A Buena Costa County Mystery

DODD, MEAD & COMPANY
New York

1 2 3 4 5 6 7 8 9 10

Library of Congress Cataloging in Publication Data

When they kill your wife.

(A Buena Costa County mystery)
I. Title.
PZ4.L9892Wh [PS3562.Y44] 813'.5'4 77-6748
ISBN 0-396-07443-X

To Jackie and Henri Coulette—
there are "only the codes"

PART ONE

You Have to Do Something

1

The thing in the morgue drawer had been a woman. A smiling face on a sunny day. A soft laugh in a dark bedroom. A woman. His wife.

"Yes," Paul Sobers said. "It's Susan."

Susan Sobers. Mrs. Paul Sobers.

"I'm sorry," Lee Beckett said. The investigator for Buena Costa County's prosecutor watched the husband. "You were separated, Mr. Sobers? Divorced?"

"She wanted to find herself," Paul Sobers said.

Six-feet-four, lean, and in his late thirties, Sobers was taller and heavier than he looked. Thin and hunched, as if he worked all day at a desk, and soft from the years at the desk. His dark hair was long on the collars of his white shirt and charcoal gray suit. His brown eyes were expressionless.

"Look what she found," he said.

"I'm sorry," Lee Beckett said again. What else did you say to a man looking at the exploded head of his wife? Beckett turned toward a desk in the corner of the morgue. "We've got some forms to fill out. We need you to sign them."

A heavy-shouldered man in his fifties, Beckett's face was burned brown, his gray hair was cropped short, and his flat blue eyes were sunk in wind creases.

"You knew who she was," Paul Sobers said. "Do you get your fun out of watching our faces when you pull out the drawer?"

"We need an identification, Sobers. It's the law."

"The law?" Sobers said. "Sometimes I think the law is the last refuge of pure savagery."

"Sometimes I agree with you," Beckett said. "Need a drink?"

Sobers looked down at the face that wasn't a face. A big bullet in the back of the head doesn't leave much face. He'd seen the work of big bullets in Viet Nam. It wasn't the same. This was . . . pretty, bright, with brains . . .

"I'll take a cigarette," Sobers said. "And those forms."

He smoked, filled in the forms, and signed them. Beckett put the forms into a drawer, lit his own cigarette.

"How long since you'd seen her, Sobers?"

"Almost a year. Married eight years, then she had to go. We didn't have children. One day she said she had to be a person. Maybe because she was thirty-four. Maybe because—" Sobers smoked, closed his eyes. "How did it—?"

"She was an X-ray technician at the Ruston Clinic. A week ago, January eighth, she worked late. They found her in the morning. One shot from a 357 Magnum, about eleven P.M. No one heard the shot. She was alone in the X-ray lab in the out-patient wing, and it's away from the main clinic. The X-ray lab's next to the pharmacy. The pharmacy was broken open; some morphine and barbiturates were gone. Sheriff Hoag's been rounding up known junkies all week. Nothing so far."

"The wrong place at the wrong time?" Sobers said.

4

"Looks that way," Beckett said. "Where were you that day?"

"Me?" Paul Sobers said. "A routine question?"

"When we called New York you weren't home. When we finally located your office, they said you had been away for two weeks."

"On business," Sobers said. "Right here in San Vicente, yes. I expect you've checked my motel by now. I was here, but I didn't see Susan, didn't call her or contact her."

Beckett smoked in the silence of the morgue.

"What do you do, Sobers?"

"Make things work right and look nice. An industrial designer, from bulldozers to fountain pens. For a big design company: Future Forms Associates. Can I go now?"

"Yeh," Beckett said. "Sobers? We'll get who did it."

Sobers seemed to look somewhere behind Beckett. "When they kill your wife, you're supposed to do something about it."

"Go home, Sobers," Beckett said.

"I don't have a home now," Paul Sobers said.

*

The Buena Costa County courthouse is a squat brick building out of step with the relentless Spanish restoration of San Vicente, the county seat—a monument to the blunt Yankees who inherited the old city by hook and crook, mostly the latter. The county prosecutor's office is on the second floor. The prosecutor, Charles Tucker, was at his desk as Beckett came in.

"How'd he take it?" Tucker asked.

"Hard," Beckett said. "She'd walked out on him a year ago, and he's going to be trouble. Unless he killed her himself."

5

Tucker pushed his papers away, sat back. He looked unhappy. Not yet forty, he was a tall, thin, intense man ready to move upward. He didn't like complications.

"Could he have?" he asked Beckett.

"He's been in San Vicente for two weeks, on a job with Electro-Micro Industries. He says he never contacted her."

"The sheriff's sure it's robbery-murder."

"A thief doesn't hit a place that's usually empty if he finds someone there. The haul was damned small, a lot of good drugs left behind . . . and junkies don't kill, they run."

"She could have been out of sight in the dark room," Tucker said. "The thief could have panicked after the killing and left loot, and junkies do kill sometimes, Lee."

Tucker looked away as he said the last. Beckett had once been a New York City police captain, until a bomb had killed his wife and son—a junkie's bomb.

"What motive would the husband have?" Tucker said.

"I'd say he still wanted her," Beckett said. "She wasn't 'finding herself' just by work, Charley. There was a man."

"Here in San Vicente? You know who?"

"Roy Butler."

"Lois Butler's brother? Our lady lawyer?" Tucker toyed with a pencil. "I'd heard he was maybe chasing Gloria Forbes."

"Yeh, so had I. Butler chases a lot of women."

Tucker got up and began to walk around the office. "You're saying someone faked the robbery to cover killing Susan Sobers? You suspect someone at Ruston's clinic?"

"Not necessarily. If I had a corpse on my hands, and the pharmacy close by, I'd think of a drug robbery for a cover."

6

"Have you talked to Hoag about it?"

"Not yet. We won't get much help from the good sheriff without a lot more to show him. He likes his murders neat. Robbery would be just right, or the husband at worst."

"Sobers had opportunity, maybe motive," Tucker said and watched Beckett. "What else? You've got more in mind."

Beckett walked to a window. "If your wife walked out on you, you still wanted her, and you were in the same town with her, would you stay away from her, Charley? Could you?"

"No," Tucker said. "I don't think I could."

"At least you'd watch from doorways," Beckett said. "Maybe he didn't kill her, but I think he knows more than he's said."

*

The apartment court was on upper Fremont Street, the main street of San Vicente, just north of the main business district. Paul Sobers waited in the warm winter sun while the manager unlocked the door. The two-story pink stucco buildings were seedy among dusty green olive and untidy lemon trees.

"She was paid the month," the manager said. "You should get something back. I'm sorry, you know? We liked her."

The manager walked away, and Paul Sobers looked at the door of where Susan had lived alone. Maybe if he had knocked on that door two weeks ago instead of hiding, watching, seeing . . .

He stood in the night across the court and watched them in the shadows of her doorway. Susan and the man . . .

Her rooms were neat and almost bare. His own photograph stood on a bureau. There was a stuffed dog he'd won for her at a carnival years ago, and some familiar

7

jewelry. But the clothes in the single closet were all new, and the shoes, and the bright underwear . . .

He watched them in her dark doorway, Susan and the man. Her skirt up above her thighs in a flash of headlights from outside the court. "No, Roy! Go to your little rich girl!" The man on her like some dark animal. "It's not the way you think, Susy. You're what I want." Locked together in her dark doorway, and then inside, her door closed, sounds . . .

Almost two weeks ago, and if he had knocked on her door, spoken in the dark, maybe . . . ?

Sobers lay on the bed in her silent bedroom. All he had done was hide in the dark and watch her—his wife. That investigator would find out, if he didn't already know. The jealous husband. Who had the man been? What had she found, Susan? What had killed her? Blind chance? Or had she found something that had killed her?

He was still thinking of what she might have found so far from him, when he heard the sound. A slow, dragging sound in the next room. *Slide . . . clump . . . slide . . . clump . . .*

The shape stood in the bedroom doorway like some optical illusion. A grizzled head barely visible above the edge of the bed where Sobers lay. The face of an old man at the height of a small boy. Sobers sat up.

"You're her husband," the face said. "Susan's old man."

Gray-haired and leathery-faced, the apparition had the chest and shoulders of a big man, but where his legs should have been there were massive leather cylinders like the feet of an elephant.

"Jack Tracy," the legless man said. He took out a burned cigar butt, lit it. "I got a room here. Susan talked about you. Said she must be crazy tradin' you for Butler. A lousy break, her gettin' killed like that."

8

"Butler?" Sobers said. "Is that his name? Her man here?"

"Roy Butler. A no-good all ways."

"You know him?"

Jack Tracy grinned. The grin made his grizzled face younger. No more than in his early sixties.

"I sells pencils down on the art museum corner. Always the same stand when I'm in San Vicente. I see them, they don't see me, you know? All cripples look the same." Tracy blew thick cigar smoke. "You talk to the sheriff?"

"A county investigator, Lee Beckett."

"Same difference, except Beckett's a real cop. You buy the way they got it worked out? Susan's killin'?"

The dwarflike man smoked. Sobers watched him.

"You don't believe it was a robbery-murder?"

"I guess the cops knows more'n I do." Tracy chewed on his cigar. "Only this Butler's a bottom-dealer, a schemer. Always into something, and on the make."

"With a 'little rich girl'?"

"You heard already, huh? Yeh, her name's Gloria Forbes. A real old family around here. Father's a lawyer, mother's a society-page blonde. The girl's a kid."

"And kids can get jealous," Sobers said. He stood up. "Where do I find these Forbes people?"

"They lives up on Mission Ridge, got a beach house down on Dawson Point," Tracy said. "If you're gonna go look, you could drop me downtown."

In his rented Impala, Sobers drove down Fremont Street toward the center of San Vicente. The day was growing hot.

"Sobers," Jack Tracy said when they reached the art museum corner, "if you go around that Roy Butler, you be careful. What I hear, he ain't no nice guy."

9

"I'll remember that," Sobers said.

He left the legless man sitting on the busy sidewalk in the sun, his tin cup and pencils spread out around him, and drove toward the harbor and his motel. In the motel room, he took a big, stubby Colt .357 from his suitcase, slipped it into his belt, and went back out to his car.

2

The Mission Ridge section of San Vicente is in the mountains that ring the narrow strip of green coast. The Forbes house, set back from a lane of tall eucalyptus trees high on the slope of a mountain, was a big Victorian frame house from the days when successful Americans in California built their homes in imitation of mansions back east.

Lee Beckett parked in the driveway. The elderly housekeeper who answered the door took him through a cool entry hall of dark wood and heavy Spanish furniture to a small rear room that was sunny with morning light. Lined from floor to ceiling on three walls with books, the room was furnished in a French style with wood-and-leather chairs and a delicate, inlaid writing desk. A woman sat at the desk.

"I'm Doris Forbes, Mr. Beckett. You wanted to talk to Gloria? May I ask why?"

Small and blonde, she was trim in a slim black suit that showed off her good legs under the open desk. Her high-boned face was flawlessly made up and her hands immaculately manicured.

11

"She's not at home?" Beckett said.

"I'm afraid not. Is it important?"

"Maybe she's at your beach house?"

"No, she—" Doris Forbes took a deep breath. "To be truthful, we don't know where she is—not for the last week."

"A week?" Beckett said. "She's run off? Some trouble?"

"If you call a man twice her age trouble, and I do."

"Roy Butler?"

"We think so." She watched Beckett. "You came here about Roy Butler, didn't you? Has he done something? Is Gloria—?"

"How old is Gloria, Mrs. Forbes?"

"Twenty."

"An older boyfriend isn't so unusual at twenty."

"Roy Butler isn't her boyfriend! He's *twenty* years older, and she's all but engaged to Peter Cole."

"Dr. Taylor's assistant over at Newmont College?"

"A steady boy, and Roy Butler's nothing but an over-age beach bum still looking for the easy pot of gold!"

"You had no warning she was going to run off?"

Doris Forbes shifted behind the small desk. "Gloria went to Newmont, and since the campus is next door to us, she lived at home. Three weeks ago she moved out to live with a friend. It seemed reasonable since it was closer to her new job in Lois Butler's law office. Gloria is thinking of being a lawyer, but now it looks like Roy Butler might have been a reason."

"How do you know she's with Butler?"

"The girl she moved in with, Janine McGrath, saw her get into his car, and no one has seen her since."

"That would have been January eighth or ninth?"

"The ninth, I think, yes."

"What have you done about it?"

"Worry," Doris Forbes said.

"You want us to look for her?"

Doris Forbes thought. "I don't want to make a mistake. At that age they think they're adults. It would be best if she returned on her own."

"Does the name Susan Sobers mean anything to you?"

"Sobers?" She frowned. "No. Should it?"

"Just a thought," Beckett said. "When you hear from Gloria, let us know, okay?"

"Of course," Doris Forbes said. "Mr. Beckett? Is it something very bad you suspect Roy Butler of doing?"

From her face, the tone of her voice, Beckett wasn't sure if she was afraid Roy Butler had done something very bad, or hoped he had.

"We don't know that he's done anything, Mrs. Forbes."

*

Paul Sobers found the beach house among palm trees on a rocky point. A beach curved away toward San Vicente. The house was a rambling stone and redwood building from a time when lumber had been cheap and labor cheaper in southern California.

As Sobers parked, a man came from behind the house and walked toward the beach. The man wore a topcoat in the sun.

There was no answer at the beach house, and no one moved inside behind the picture window. Sobers knocked again, listened to the empty echo, and walked toward the beach. In the distance the man in the topcoat sat alone on a rock with his back against a low bluff, looking out toward the open sea.

"Mr. Forbes?" Paul Sobers asked as he reached the man.

The man had a pleasant face with no special features. Detached and distant, he sat watching the ocean. He wore black-rimmed glasses over blue, distracted eyes and hunched in his topcoat.

13

"What? Yes, Henry Forbes. I'm sorry, do we—?"

"No, you don't know me," Sobers said. "My name is Paul Sobers. I'm looking for your daughter Gloria. I'd like to talk to her about—"

"Sobers?" Henry Forbes stared at Sobers with something like shock on his distracted face and looked past Sobers at the same time—as if there were two different men behind his pale blue eyes. "You're a relative of Susan Sobers?"

"She was my wife," Sobers said.

"Wife?" Henry Forbes went on staring out to sea as if the answer to some question were out there. "I'm very sorry. Yes, very sorry."

"You knew Susan?"

Forbes nodded. "At Ruston's clinic. We talked a few times. So senseless, you know? We live in a senseless world."

"Did your daughter know Susan? Maybe better than just at the clinic?"

"Gloria? No, I don't think so."

"Can I talk to her? Gloria?"

"She's away . . . out of town."

"Will she be away long?"

"Long?" Distracted again, detached, looking at something that wasn't there. "I don't really know. Perhaps my wife . . ."

Forbes trailed off. Up the beach three girls and two boys ran from the picnic area, sank down laughing on the sand. Two in bikinis and one in a slim white tank suit, the girls sat on their heels, their upper bodies held erect to display their flat bellies and high young breasts. The boys lay on their backs, hands behind their heads to emphasize their arm muscles, deep chests, and narrow loins.

"Do you know a Roy Butler?" Paul Sobers asked.

14

"Damned lecher!" Henry Forbes said.

"He's after your daughter?"

Forbes looked toward the adolescents up the beach, looked out to sea, isolated like a man under a glass bell. "She was always a good kid, Gloria. No trouble, always laughing. And smart, really bright. She'll have a good life, do well. A head on her shoulders, steady. She'll be someone."

"Did you know that Roy Butler was seeing my wife?"

"Was he?" He stood up. "I'm sorry, I have some work."

Paul Sobers watched Forbes walk away along the beach, still hunched inside his topcoat in the warm sun.

*

Doris Forbes stood at a narrow front window of her old house, looking out over the city. She held a martini. A man sat on the sofa behind her.

"I always wanted to put in a glass front. With our view, it's a crime to keep these old windows. Remodeled, the house would be worth ten times as much. Henry wouldn't do it."

"It doesn't matter, Doris," the man said.

Doris Forbes drank. "Where *is* Gloria, Russ?"

"I hope not with Roy Butler," Dr. Russell Taylor said.

A stocky man, about forty, he had only a touch of gray in his dark hair. His suit was conservative, with vest and watch chain, and he had a quick, confident face. A mature man, smooth and vigorous-looking.

"That cheap parasite!" Doris Forbes drained her martini. "There was a man here from Tucker's office, a Lee Beckett. He asked about Gloria and Roy Butler and someone named Sobers."

"Susan Sobers," Taylor said. "That X-ray technician killed in the robbery at Ruston's clinic." He only sipped at his martini. "Could Roy Butler have known her?"

15

"I wouldn't be too surprised, Russ. Could the police be thinking it wasn't really a robbery?"

"Possibly. When does Henry leave?"

"Tonight."

"Shouldn't you start looking for Gloria?"

"I'll give her a few more days. Henry should be away at least two weeks, perhaps longer."

"He did go to Los Angeles a few days ago?"

"Yes, of course."

"I hope so," Russell Taylor said.

*

Paul Sobers had lunch in a Mexican restaurant, then drove up to Mission Ridge and parked in the Forbes's driveway behind a red Mercedes two-seater and a brown Continental Mark IV. He got out and stood in the warm, shaded silence of the rich suburb.

The big, white, three-story Forbes house was set on a narrow lawn surrounded by the brown and dusty-green natural growth of southern California. Susan would have liked it—aristocratic and solidly affluent. The next house was vaguely visible to the right, and to the left untouched chaparral stretched a quarter of a mile to the campus of a small college. Behind the house, the land sloped up to a ridge that overlooked the college. A stone tower stood on the crest.

A spectacular view of the sea and the city spread far below, but without constant watering it was all dry, steep land that would have sold for pennies a hundred years ago. The Spanish *rancheros* had preferred their in-land canyons for cattle. This ridge had been built up by baronial Yankees who had wanted their big houses to be seen and admired.

The housekeeper who took Sobers' name into Mrs. Forbes led him into a high-ceilinged living room. The furniture was Victorian, and the walls had yellowed. A worn old room, but the couple drinking cocktails were neither worn nor old. The woman came to meet him. She was slender and poised and looked to be in her thirties.

"Mr. Sobers? You're a relative of that poor woman who was—?"

"My wife," he said.

"I'm so sorry. Is there something we can do?"

She looked up at Sobers. There was something soft about her even in the tailored black suit. A sculptured face.

"You knew Susan, Mrs. Forbes?"

"No, I didn't. But I think Russ there did. Mr. Sobers, Dr. Russell Taylor."

The men shook hands. Taylor made Sobers think of an evangelist or a gambler. He wasn't sure why, unless it was that the man was so smoothly confident and that on his watch chain he wore what looked like a Phi Beta Kappa key but wasn't.

"I only knew her at Ruston's clinic," Taylor said. "Is something on your mind, Mr. Sobers?"

"A man named Roy Butler," Sobers said. "I think he's a friend of Mrs. Forbes's daughter, and I've heard that Gloria is out of town. I was wondering if she could be with Butler?"

"I hope not," Doris Forbes said.

Russell Taylor said, "Gloria deserves better than Butler. She and my assistant, Peter Cole, are essentially engaged."

"Russ is president of Newmont College next door to us," Doris Forbes said. "He's very close to Gloria and Peter."

"But Gloria isn't with this Peter?"

"No," Doris Forbes said.

Taylor said, "I have to leave, Doris. Tonight?"

17

"At seven, Russ."

After Taylor had gone, Doris Forbes stood staring at a mirror on the wall. She touched her blonde hair.

"How old are you, Mr. Sobers?"

"Thirty-seven."

She nodded, and he suddenly guessed that she knew his age, height, and weight within a hair. Aware of men. And older than she seemed. A woman who worked to stay youthful, and under the slim body there had once been a rounder girl.

"Gloria lives at home?" Sobers asked.

"She did. A few weeks ago she took a job in Lois Butler's law office and moved in with a girl from the office, Janine McGrath. I suppose it made it easier to be around Roy. Lois is his sister. Not that she'd want him around Gloria any more than I do."

"Or Dr. Taylor?"

"Russ is an old friend. In a way he got Gloria and Peter Cole together. His two prize students, the perfect match."

"What does Cole think about her and Butler?"

"I don't imagine he likes it."

"Where does Roy Butler live?"

"Out of a suitcase!" Her voice was bitter. "He pays more for his car than he does for rent."

"When did Gloria go away?"

"About a week ago, January ninth."

It was the day after Susan had been shot.

"Mrs. Forbes?" Sobers said. "Is Gloria missing? Has she disappeared? Run away?"

Doris Forbes drank her martini. "I don't know."

3

Paul Sobers watched Doris Forbes drive away in the red Mercedes. He got out of his Impala, leaving it parked in the shaded lane, and slipped up to the rear of the old house. He found the rear door open and went up the back stairs. The upper floors were still and silent.

Gloria's room, a large room with a ceiling that sloped down to a window seat, was on the third floor. It had the aura of a hideaway, the room of a child who reads books alone and lies awake at night full of secret dreams.

The stuffed animals of childhood stood on low shelves. There were snapshots of nine-year-olds hugging each other, and stiff high school photographs. Adolescent keepsakes yellowed around the bureau mirror, and academic prizes were displayed on shelves. Gloria Forbes's whole past was in the room, but it wasn't a room that belonged to the past. The present was alive, too.

The desk was cluttered with current projects, books and magazines on politics and history. There was woman's make-up and closets full of clothes. Two framed photos showed a serious young man with an intense face and a shy smile. One was a portrait signed

Love, Peter. In the other the same young man stood with a girl who had to be Gloria Forbes herself.

She was taller than her mother, dark-haired and full-bodied, but not heavy. A big girl, with a Celtic face and smiling eyes. Alert and serious, but not rebellious. The face of someone who's recent dreams were of the possible in a real world.

Sobers searched through the room for anything that might relate to Roy Butler, or to Susan. He found nothing. Then he found the poem. Crudely typed, it was under her pillow:

> If I were travelling on the moon
> they would hear me, call my name
> across the frozen mountains
> and the sand.
>
> So many forgotten voices.
>
> Turn away then, unaware
> the emerald cat clutched
> to your private breast
> is dead.

There was no author's name, and Sobers was reading the poem again when the door of the room opened behind him. Henry Forbes stood in the doorway.

"I'm sorry. I heard. . . . What are you—?"

He seemed confused, as if afraid he'd forgotten something he'd been told. Sobers took a chance.

"Your wife let me look at Gloria's room."

"Oh, yes. Of course."

Sobers said, "Does Gloria write poetry?"

"Poetry? No, I don't think so. I . . ." Forbes blinked.

"I heard noise up here. I thought that—"

"That Gloria might have come home?"

"I hoped . . ." His voice trailed off.

Sobers held out the typed poem. "Did you ever see this before? She must have copied it from somewhere."

Forbes looked at the poem. "No, I never saw it. Well, I'm afraid I have to go and pack."

"You're going somewhere?"

"A business trip."

"What business is that, Mr. Forbes?"

"Calixco Petroleum." Forbes blinked again, like an old owl in a foggy night. "She'll be all right, have a good life."

Alone in the silent room, Sobers listened to Forbes going down to the second floor. Parent and child. The parent must try to keep the child safe. The child must break away, take risks. Both were right. He, Sobers, had never had a child, and what did a husband do when a wife had to break away?

He looked toward the photograph of Gloria and Peter Cole. What did an almost-fiancé do when his woman broke away?

*

Peter Cole climbed the open stairs of an office building on Cota Street. One of those California office buildings that look more like haciendas, with every office opening onto an outside gallery. The last office on the second floor was that of Lois Butler, Attorney. Cole went in.

He was a short youth, and his thin face lacked that façade of inner certainty, real or fake, that made a man. His hair was short and proper, and his dark suit had no identity. A round-faced blonde receptionist began an automatic smile as he entered the office, and then scowled.

"Peter, I told you—"

"I thought maybe Miss Butler might have heard from her."

"She hasn't, and neither have I."

"It's been a week! Where'd she go?"

"If I knew anything, I'd tell you."

"Maybe I don't believe you, Janine."

"You don't own her! Not Gloria."

"No," Cole said bitterly. "We're not even really engaged."

Janine McGrath's voice softened. "She'll come home, Peter."

He left the office slowly and went down to his small Ford. Books were piled on the front seat. He drove up to Newmont College on Mission Ridge, parked at the library, but didn't get out. He sat there in his car in the early evening sun.

Then he started the car again and drove off the campus toward the ocean and the beach.

*

By the time Paul Sobers had shaved, showered, eaten his dinner at a franchise steak house, and looked up Janine McGrath's address, it was dark in San Vicente.

The address was a garden apartment on the West Side, with three rows of units around a pool. Janine McGrath lived on a corner of the second floor. Sobers got no answer from her dark unit. He took off his jacket, wrapped his hand in it, broke a windowpane, and unlocked the window.

Inside there was a living room, kitchen, dining alcove, one bedroom, and a bathroom. Neither twin bed had been used. The larger closet was full of clothes too small for Gloria Forbes. In the second closet there were two office dresses in a larger size, a pair of jeans, and a suitcase. The suitcase was full of dirty clothes, some books, and three letters.

The letters were to Gloria from Roy Butler, with a San Vicente return address on Miramar Beach. Two were long, torrid, and dated in November. The third was short, dated just over three weeks ago, and said that Butler had to see her to tell her something very important.

The books were two novels and a thin volume of poems. The poet was named John Glavin, the book had been published a year ago in New York by a Virgo Press, and the first poem in the book was the one Gloria Forbes had had under her pillow. There was no dust jacket, no biography of the poet, and the last poem sounded a lot like the first to Sobers:

> It is time to understand
> what we are.
> Animals with thumbs
> opposed,
> guided by hungers and chance,
> formed by accident.
>
> Those who have
> prefer injustice to disorder.
> Those who have not suffer
> disorder before denial.
> Most,
> who neither have nor have not,
> play cards and dream
> of openings and hands,
> are not concerned
> with justice,
> or disorder,
> or those who have or have not.

23

A lot like the first poem and yet different. More detached, objective. The work of an older man, as if the poems covered a long span of time.

Sobers sat in the living room of the small apartment with the book of poems and Roy Butler's last letter. The poems had obviously meant something to Gloria Forbes, and just over three weeks ago Butler had had something important he wanted to tell her. Three weeks ago Gloria Forbes had moved out of her home. A week ago . . .

Out on the gallery someone was coming toward the apartment—lurching toward the apartment, banging and crashing into the wall and railing. Someone who stopped outside the closed door, rattled the knob violently, and suddenly hurled against the door.

Sobers jumped into the bedroom, slipped behind the inner door. He took out his gun. The unseen force slammed into the outer door again, and it burst open with a ripping of wood.

Grunts and hoarse breathing like some large animal out in the small living room. Furniture crashed over. Glass and wood smashed to the floor. Sobers, his gun in his hand, peered out into the living room.

A massive bear of a man snorted and shuffled through the small living room, searching. Too large for the room, he knocked things off tables, swept objects to the floor, at every motion. Shaggy, he had shoulder-length gray hair, a full beard, and wore a dirty denim jacket and jeans. His belly hung over the jeans, but it wasn't soft. Sobers could think only of those mountain men in western movies who rumble out of the snow with hands big enough to break a man's back.

Sobers stepped from the bedroom. He had his gun.

"What do you want here? Who are you?"

The giant stopped in his search, looked. Red, liquid eyes in the shaggy face looked at Sobers. Smiled. An almost dreamy smile through the heavy beard. A soft laugh:

"Hey . . . hey, man . . ."

Moved with the speed of a grizzly.

Sobers tried to raise his gun. He was too slow.

The giant had the gun, reached out . . .

*

Sobers sat on a floor with his head against a wall. In a bright, silent room—the same room, in Janine McGrath's living room. His jaw ached, and he remembered the massive man moving. He didn't remember anything else. He got up slowly. His pistol was on the floor. He picked it up . . . and jumped back, shaking!

A shadow loomed in the broken doorway.

"Gloria?"

A smaller man, younger, without hair on his thin face. Sobers recognized him—Peter Cole. Cole stared at the gun.

"Who . . . who are you?"

"Paul Sobers. Maybe you know the name, Cole? Sobers? Susan Sobers? The woman murdered in Ruston's Clinic?"

"I never heard of her!" Cole cried.

The short, solemn-looking young man still stared at the gun in Sober's hand, then looked slowly around the room.

"A . . . a big man came out. Did he do this?"

"Was the man Roy Butler?"

"God, no! Butler's blond and handsome."

Peter Cole said the word *handsome* as if he knew he wasn't. Yet he was. An uncertain youth, without confidence.

"You expected Gloria Forbes to be here?" Sobers said.

Cole nodded. "I went to the beach house. Mr. Forbes was there, but I couldn't make him hear me. He was

25

playing music and drinking. I thought maybe that meant Gloria was back."

"You're sure she's coming back?"

Cole seemed to flinch as if slapped. His voice was angry.

"We decided to hang loose." His lips almost sneered at the youth jargon. "I guess Butler can be exciting to a girl. A Hollywood actor once, been everywhere. But she *knew* he was an inch deep, a chaser! She only went on seeing him because Mr. and Mrs. Forbes told her not to. That made her mad, but she dropped him back in November. I thought she had, anyway." Cole shook his head, unhappy. "She was funny the last weeks. Said we were just stupid kids, then ran off."

"What did you do about it?"

"Waited, what else?" Peter Cole said. "We all did, except Mr. Forbes. He looked all over town, even came to me. He went out of town one day looking for her, I guess."

"Where?" Sobers said. "Where did Forbes look?"

"I don't know."

Sobers watched the youth. Neither Forbes nor his wife had said anything about Forbes looking for Gloria. Maybe Doris Forbes didn't know. Now Forbes was going away again, and drinking alone in his beach house.

"Let's go and talk to Forbes," Sobers said.

The young man nodded, went out. Sobers put his gun away, looked for the book of poems to take with him. He looked all around the shattered room. The book wasn't there.

Slowly, he followed Peter Cole out.

*

On Dawson Point, only the Forbes house showed light in the January night. Light and music. No one answered their knocking.

26

Through the window, Sobers saw a bottle on a coffee table and records piled on an automatic turntable. The music was heavy, symphonic. Sobers saw the overturned chair half hidden by a couch. He broke a side window, climbed inside.

Henry Forbes lay between a desk and the overturned chair, a big gun near his hand. The pool of blood was still wet.

A single glass stood on the desk. A note pad and pen lay beside it. A real pen, uncapped and ready to write. But there was nothing written on the note pad. Sobers saw the photograph on the floor under the desk.

Dirty and wrinkled, it showed Gloria Forbes and a man in bathing suits on the deck of a beach house. The man was so handsome it was hard to believe he was real. The smile on his face was automatic, as if he smiled for any camera.

"Roy Butler," Peter Cole said. "That's his beach house."

Sobers picked up the telephone and called the sheriff.

4

Deputies and coroner's men crowded through the beach house. Paul Sobers sat in a corner. He thought about Susan. Was this how it had been for her, too? Her blind eyes in a pool of her own blood, the hands of the coroner on her soft body, the feet of strangers stepping over her as if she had never existed?

"I told you to go home," Lee Beckett said.

They had taken Peter Cole into another room, had sent for Doris Forbes, and Beckett had told the sheriff's deputies who Sobers was. The sheriff was out of town, and Beckett had taken charge. Sobers had told him about seeing Henry and Doris Forbes, about the giant in Janine McGrath's apartment, and about finding Henry Forbes in the locked beach house.

"My wife was murdered," Sobers said. "Now Forbes."

"Don't play detective, Sobers! You hear?"

"Someone killed my wife. Maybe it was just a robbery, but something's going on around here." He held out the wrinkled snapshot. "I found it under his desk, near his body. Gloria and Roy Butler. Why would Forbes have wanted a picture of his daughter and Roy Butler—a man he hated to be near her?"

"Maybe to show people. Cole says he was looking for her."

"It's dirty, crumpled, as if it's been carried loose in a pocket or a handbag for a long time. Forbes was looking for Gloria less than a week. Who was he showing it to here?"

"How do you think it got here, Sobers?" Beckett said. "Maybe dropped out of a pocket or handbag while pulling something else out—like a big gun. Gloria could have had it, or Butler, or anyone. Even Peter Cole. He was here earlier, and it's the kind of picture a jilted boyfriend just might keep to cry over, suffer better. Anyone, except Forbes. He's the last man I'd expect to have a picture like that."

"Unless it was just in the house. Gloria does live here, Sobers," Beckett said drily. "Or maybe Henry Forbes just had to take a last look at his daughter. You know?"

Sobers was silent. "You mean suicide."

"One shot in the right temple at close range. An hour or so before you found him. No struggle, no other marks on him, only one used glass, and the house is locked up tight. A note pad on the desk next to his glass, his pen open and ready to write. Gun, chair, and body in the right places."

"Except he didn't write any note," Sobers said.

Beckett stood up. "Go back to your motel, Sobers. Stay there. Stay in town now, but stop being a detective. I mean it this time."

Paul Sobers got up. "If Forbes put that note pad and pen on his desk, why didn't he write the note, Beckett?"

"Maybe he found he had nothing left he wanted to say," Lee Beckett said.

*

"He didn't kill himself," Doris Forbes said.

She stood in the glaring living room and looked down at the body of her husband. She looked away. Dr. Russell Taylor and another man were behind her. She twisted a pair of white gloves in her hands. The hands and her slim body shook.

"I'm sorry, Mrs. Forbes," Beckett said.

"He had no reason. None!"

"Sit down, Mrs. Forbes," Beckett said.

She sat in a straight chair, her knees together under a long green evening dress skin tight to her slim hips.

"We'll investigate," Beckett said, "but everything fits suicide. The gun was in the right place, only his prints on it. The chair is where it would be if he'd been sitting in it when. . . . The glass is right for a man drinking alone while making up his mind. The windows are all locked, and both doors. There's no sign of a break-in, no unexplained tracks outside, no struggle, no search, and no evidence of anyone else."

"No," Doris Forbes said. She sat on the edge of her chair as if afraid of breaking through the crust of the earth.

Beckett showed her the gun. "You know this gun?"

She looked at the big pistol, looked away.

"It's Henry's gun," Dr. Russell Taylor admitted. "Have you considered a thief, a prowler? Some of those wild-animal youths? This house is on the beach; transients and vagrant kids are always camping out there, prowling."

"No break in, no search, no theft," Beckett said.

There was a silence in the glare of the room, and Doris Forbes reached up to hold Russell Taylor's hand.

"You two were together tonight?" Beckett said. "Where?"

"At the Bistro," Taylor said. "We're known there,

Beckett. I'm sure we were seen."

"You two see each other a lot?"

"Now you listen, Beckett! I don't—" Taylor began.

Beckett shook his head. "I don't care what you two do or don't do. I just wonder what Forbes might have cared about?"

"Dr. Taylor and I are friends!" Doris Forbes cried. "We work for his college. We . . . we . . ." Her voice ran down like a dying engine. Her hands became still. "No, I won't pretend. Henry and I didn't have the best of marriages. There have been men, quite a few. Not Russ, but I suppose Henry could have misunderstood. I don't apologize, and Henry really never cared about other men. He cared that our marriage wasn't good, but not about other men, and he wouldn't kill himself for that."

"What would he kill himself for?" Beckett said.

The second man who had come in with Doris Forbes stepped forward. His voice was firm, authoritative:

"I think that's enough now, Beckett."

"A medical opinion, Dr. Ruston?" Beckett said.

"If you give her some time," Dr. Martin Ruston said, "I'm sure she'll be more help."

Ruston was a stout man with a crisp, executive manner. He had the affluent look of a successful businessman, and he wasn't pleased. Not the kind of doctor who made house calls or saw a patient without a referral. Ruston's patients wouldn't walk in off the street, and his manner was both brisk and careful.

"As her doctor," Ruston said, "I must insist she go home and rest."

"Were you Henry Forbes's doctor, too, Dr. Ruston?" Beckett asked.

"Yes, I was."

"Can you give us any reason for suicide?"

"No, I can't," Dr. Ruston snapped. "Russ is right, look

for a prowler. No one is safe these days, as I know too well."

"Your robbery at the clinic," Beckett said, nodded. "But there was no robbery here, was there?"

*

Paul Sobers sat in the Impala listening to the voices inside the house. Had Susan ever come here? His stomach felt hollow and sick. Did a man ever get over it, the sickness at the thought of his wife with another man?

The car stopped up the road in a grove of trees. A flame flared, and a cigarette began to glow. Sobers took out his gun, circled through the trees.

"Does a gun make you feel manly?"

A woman's voice inside the car. She switched on the light. A tall woman in a green silk suit, mannish but not masculine. In her thirties, Sobers guessed. She had a full body, short copper hair, and steady eyes. A bold face, severe, and handsome rather than pretty. A familiar face to Sobers—a female version of Roy Butler.

"Miss Butler?" Sobers said.

"Counsellor," she said. "It avoids the matrimonial status problem. Who are you?"

"Paul Sobers. My wife—"

"Yes, I remember."

"You came to see Henry Forbes, Counsellor?"

"You say *Counsellor* as if it hurts. Make it *Miss* then, I don't really care. Is he dead?"

"Yes."

She nodded. "I know the coroner's van. Murder?"

"Lee Beckett thinks suicide."

"You don't, Mr. Sobers?"

"Where are Gloria Forbes and your brother, Miss Butler?"

"Like that?" Lois Butler thought for a time, a good lawyer. "Gloria was disturbed when I saw her last, and

32

my brother is unpredictable. Henry had been looking for them, upset. An explosive mixture, but Gloria and Roy aren't murderers."

"Could they be back in San Vicente?"

"I couldn't say."

"Can you say anything about why Forbes would kill himself?"

"No," Lois Butler said.

At the beach house they were all coming out. Lois Butler got out of her car, and walked toward them. There was nothing mannish about her walk. She went to Doris Forbes.

"Terrible," she said. "Can I do anything, Doris?"

"Do?" Doris Forbes's blonde hair was dishevelled, her face hollow. "It looks like I've done enough, doesn't it? Indulging myself while Henry. . . . That's what they think." She stared past Lois Butler into the dark windows of her red Mercedes the way she had stared into the mirror on the wall of her big house. "They're wrong. They're terribly wrong."

"I'll give you a sedative," Dr. Martin Ruston said.

Ruston helped Doris Forbes into the Mercedes and got in himself on the driver's side. They drove away. Russell Taylor walked to Lois Butler.

"Mind taking me home, Lois?" Taylor said, smiled.

"My pleasure," she said.

"Or perhaps a drink? I feel like company, I think."

"A drink sounds just fine, Russ," Lois Butler said.

Peter Cole went alone to his small Ford.

*

The old beach house was silent on its rocky point, although in the distance the sound of traffic on the freeway to the north and the surge of the surf on the beach to the south could be heard. Lee Beckett sat on the couch with his eyes closed. Paul Sobers stood against a far wall.

"Taylor and Doris Forbes were having an affair?" Paul Sobers said. "Forbes found out? That's it?"

Beckett didn't move or open his eyes on the couch. "I told you to go away, to stay away from this."

"You didn't tell me how," Sobers said.

On the couch, Beckett remained motionless for another few moments. Then he opened his eyes. He looked at the pool of blood on the floor—dried blood now.

"Taylor's got a woman. Has had for years," he said.

"Lois Butler?"

"They've been pretty discreet. Newmont is a religious college," Beckett said. "Nothing says, though, he wouldn't like two women. A power man, big fish in a medium-sized pond. Maybe he was even more discreet with Doris Forbes, and maybe that was too much for Henry Forbes. Maybe that's what Roy Butler had to tell Gloria. And maybe it's why Gloria ran off."

Twenty-year-old girls could be rigid, especially where their mothers were involved, Sobers knew. A big shock for some children to discover that their parents have passions, needs.

"My wife just a robbery victim after all," Sobers said, "and Forbes a suicide because of his wife. Nothing to do with Roy Butler or Gloria?"

Beckett said nothing, closed his eyes again on the couch.

"If Butler married Gloria," Sobers said, "what could he expect to get when the parents died?"

"I don't know. But it was suicide, Sobers. Period."

"All right, suicide, but are you sure of the reason?" Sobers said. "My wife was killed a week ago, the eighth. Gloria ran off a week ago, the ninth. I don't like that much coincidence."

"Be a cop, you'll find out."

"Susan worked at Ruston's Clinic. Ruston is the

Forbes family doctor. Gloria ran off the day after Susan died—with a man who was involved with Susan. Henry Forbes went looking for Gloria and Butler. Now he's dead, too."

"A suicide," Beckett said.

"But perhaps not over his wife. Perhaps his looking for Gloria was the reason for suicide."

Beckett opened his eyes, looked at Sobers.

"What reason?" he said.

"Maybe he found Gloria," Sobers said.

Beckett went on looking at Sobers for a time, then closed his eyes again, and sat unmoving on the couch. Sobers left.

In his rented car, Sobers drove back into San Vicente and his motel. He got a beer and sat in the dark room thinking about Gloria and Henry Forbes. Had Forbes found Gloria—and found something he couldn't go on living with?

5

Paul Sobers woke up thinking of Doris Forbes. The wife
—widow, now—had been insistent that Henry Forbes
couldn't have committed suicide. Because she was sure
he hadn't, or because she was afraid he had?

He showered and shaved, had some toast and coffee,
and drove back to Janine McGrath's apartment. The
January morning sun was clear and cool, and the parking
lot behind the apartment units was empty except for a
green station wagon with a man working under it.

Janine McGrath wasn't home again. The window was
still broken, and inside the rooms had been straightened
but were as empty as last night. Sobers went back down
to his car. Janine McGrath was probably at work. In the
parking lot, the man under the green station wagon
crawled out. Sobers stopped.

It was the big, bearlike man of last night. He stretched
his back, smiled through his beard toward Sobers without any recognition. Sobers moved his hand toward the
pistol tucked in his belt under his jacket. The big man
knew the movement.

"Cop?" He blinked his red-rimmed eyes. His voice was

light and hoarse, like someone hit too often in the throat. In the daylight his eyes were light blue, and under the gray beard he had a rough, square face with a long scar from his right eye to his right ear. He still wore the dirty denim jeans and jacket, but in the daylight there was nothing of the snuffling animal about him. His face behind all the hair had a lively intelligence, the blue eyes were bright and even sensitive, and there was nothing wary, only curious.

"Why did you attack me last night?" Sobers demanded. He kept his hand near his gun. He remembered the speed and skill of those massive hands.

"Attack?" He seemed puzzled. "Me?"

"I tried to talk to you, you knocked me cold."

"It's news to me. Why would I do that?"

"You were searching Janine McGrath's apartment."

He shook his leonine head. "I guess I don't remember doing anything last night." He kicked the ground, sheepish. "I drink some. Sorry, you know? I'm Frank Kapek, Mr. . . .? Or is it lieutenant?"

"Paul Sobers, and it's just mister."

"Yeh," he said. "What was I looking for up there?"

"A book of poems, I think. You took the book."

He nodded. "I kind of wondered how I got the book back. I thought maybe Gloria gave it back, and I forgot."

"You always forget what you do when you're drunk?"

"Not always," Frank Kapek said.

"You know Gloria Forbes well?"

"Just a neighbor."

"Why would you want her book of poems?"

"It's my book; I lent it to her. She liked it." He was proud that Gloria Forbes had liked John Glavin's poems.

"You know where Gloria is now?"

"She hasn't been around. Maybe for a week."

"You read a lot of poetry, Mr. Kapek?"

"Frank, okay?" He smiled. "I don't look like a poetry buff, yeh? Well I am. I read a lot. They taught me how to read in school, but I learned what to read in the joint. You got plenty of time to read when you're inside."

"Prison?" Sobers said. "For what?"

Kapek stiffened. It wasn't anger, more a kind of reserve. The question wasn't good manners. Kapek was polite.

"You name it, I did it," he said.

"Did you have a special reason to give Gloria the poems?"

"I get anyone I can to read Johnny Glavin's poems," Kapek said. "We were in Soledad together eleven years ago. He was a hell of a poet, but the joint broke him—rehabilitated him until he didn't know who he was anymore. When he got out, he stopped writing, got sick, and died. That was back in 1966. His friends sort of kept him alive, got his book out last year. I give it to everyone."

"What was Glavin in prison for?"

"Manslaughter." Kapek shrugged. "A fight, the guy died."

"Could Glavin have meant something to Gloria Forbes?"

"Far as I know she never heard of him."

"Did she have many visitors here?"

"I don't know. Her old man came looking for her once."

"What did he say?"

"Asked if I knew where she was. If I knew a Roy Butler."

"You'd met Henry Forbes before?"

"No." Kapek watched Sobers. "Something happen to him?"

"He was shot last night. The police think suicide."

Kapek ran his big hand through his beard. "What did

Camus say? 'The way the world is, any rational man has to kill himself?' Something like that. Tolstoy, too; 'If life isn't infinite, it's absurd, and we must rid ourselves of it as soon as possible by committing suicide.' "

Enormous and hairy in his dirty denims, he looked like a hobo, but he could quote Camus and Tolstoy, and seemed to feel pain in the January sun for a man he hadn't known.

"You do read a lot," Sobers said.

"Yeh, but what do I know? 'Give life a meaning that can't be taken away by death.' Tolstoy again."

"A nice thought," Sobers said.

"But who lets you do it?" Kapek said. He seemed shaken. By the death of a stranger? "You see Gloria, you tell her Frank Kapek's sorry."

As he drove away, Sobers looked back. Frank Kapek had a bottle, took a long drink.

*

In Lois Butler's law office, Janine McGrath looked up as Lee Beckett came in.

"I'm sorry, Counsellor isn't in, Mr. Beckett."

"You heard about Henry Forbes, Janine?"

She nodded. "Why did he do it?"

"His wife doesn't think he did do it."

"She doesn't think. . . . You mean . . . murder?"

Beckett said, "Is Gloria back in town yet, Janine?"

"No!" she cried. "I mean, I don't know."

"You know your apartment was searched. Why didn't you report that to us?"

She started to cry. "Was it you? I . . . I was scared. I don't want to get mixed up in all of it! I just let Gloria move in, and now she's gone, her father's dead, and someone wrecked my apartment!"

"Mixed up in all of what, Janine?"

"I don't know! Gloria was crazy before she ran off. Mr.

39

Forbes was frantic to find her. He scared me."

"All right," Beckett said. "We didn't search your place. It was a big, bearded man." Beckett described the man Paul Sobers had reported.

"I know him! I mean, he lives in my building, drives a green station wagon. I never talked to him, but I think Gloria did. She was home a lot before she ran off."

"He seems to have taken a book of poems Gloria had. Did Gloria ever talk about John Glavin or his poetry?"

"She even read me some. I didn't like them."

"You said she was acting crazy. You know why? Had she met anyone new? Did she ever mention a Susan Sobers?"

"Sobers? No, and no one came around except Roy, and Peter, and Mrs. Forbes once."

"Was Peter Cole jealous of Butler? Did they fight?"

"Peter never fights. I don't know if he was jealous."

"Could Gloria have killed her father, Janine?"

Beckett slipped it out and watched Janine McGrath. The girl shrank back, guilty, and too slow to cover.

"They . . . they had a terrible fight the day before she went off. On the beach. I'd taken a walk, and they didn't see me come back. Gloria screamed at Mr. Forbes. About lies and cheating and hate. I was up the beach, didn't hear much, but Gloria was shaking, and Mr. Forbes was white."

She stopped, seemed to be seeing again the violent scene on the open beach.

"Call us if you see her," Beckett said.

*

Around the corner of the open gallery, Paul Sobers hid until Beckett had gone. He didn't go into Lois Butler's office. He'd heard it all, and Janine McGrath wouldn't tell him any more.

In his Impala, he drove out to Miramar Beach on the

edge of San Vicente. A long row of house were directly on the beach, with garages at the rear and windows facing the sea. A large hotel was across the road from the beach and the houses.

Roy Butler's house was the one in the snapshot under Henry Forbes's desk. Two stories and narrow, it had a high window facing the ocean and a closed deck above the garage in the rear. No one answered Sobers' knock. The front door was open.

The living room reached back to a dining room and the kitchen, all the rooms the full width of the narrow house. A circular staircase went up to the second floor. An elegant house, but rented out, the furniture sparse and cheap.

"Who's down there? Roy?"

It was a woman's voice from upstairs.

"Paul Sobers!" he called up.

There was a momentary silence. "Come up, Mr. Sobers. Rear deck."

He went up and through a bare bedroom out onto the closed rear deck. Lois Butler sat in a chair working on some papers.

"Drink?" she said. "Or is it too early?"

She stood and went to a home bar. She wore only the bottom of a white bikini. Her breasts swung loose and white between her tanned belly and shoulders.

"Maybe a beer," Sobers said.

She got a bottle of beer from the bar refrigerator. Her hips were wide and solid. She poured the beer into a glass, gave it to Sobers, and saw his eyes looking at her breasts.

"I don't like my breasts confined," she said.

"They're your breasts," Sobers said.

"Yes, they are."

"Why bother to wear the bottom?"

"Because I choose to! I'm sorry if bare breasts disturb you. It's how I like to dress at home."

"Bare breasts on a handsome woman affect me, Miss Butler. They affect most men. I'm sorry if that disturbs you."

She drank. The motion made her breasts swing heavy.

"Men are going to have to learn to control that, Paul. This isn't the Stone Age."

"That sounds good to me."

"It does?"

"If bare breasts didn't affect men," Sobers said, "then men would be free."

She frowned, looked down at her full breasts.

"I'm not sure I want men to be that free."

"I'm sure that you don't," Sobers said.

She turned to refill her drink. She was hard and firm for a woman over thirty, and Sobers imagined her working out in some gym just like any lawyer. When she turned back, he suddenly felt that she was more aware of her breasts, or more aware of him, or both.

"You thought I was Roy," he said. "So he is in town?"

"I called his name because who else would walk into this house?" She drank. "I expect you came for a reason?"

"Are Russell Taylor and Doris Forbes having an affair?"

"Why ask me?"

"I hear you're close to Taylor yourself."

She nodded. "For some years. I don't know why. He's stiff and narrow, preaches duty and service, and believes what he says or he wouldn't be president of Newmont. Sometimes he can barely squeeze time for me. I don't see him trying to juggle two women."

"Where is Roy, Lois?"

"I don't know."

42

"But you think he's with Gloria Forbes?"

"It seems so."

"Why? Does Gloria have money?"

"She's a girl, Paul, a conquest."

"Is Roy the type for conquests with nothing extra?"

"Roy is for any conquest," she said.

She stood so close to him that she had to tilt her head back to look at his face. There was something about a woman naked while he was dressed. Or maybe he'd been alone too long.

"Would you like to look at his bedroom?" she said. "It might tell you something."

It was the front bedroom with the view of the beach and the sea. The double bed was unmade. She stood over the bed and looked out at some distant surfers. Her heavy breasts rose and fell softly with her deep breathing.

"They ride in and out all day," she said.

She watched the surfers far out, but Sobers felt what she wanted. The free future wasn't quite yet for her. She wanted him to take her—stop her talking, strip her, take her to the bed. The Stone Age. But he didn't move, not ready, and he felt the moment pass. She smiled and touched his chest with one finger, as if saying that the moment would come again.

"Have another beer on the deck," she said.

She turned her back to have him tie on her bikini top. He tied it. She went down and out the front door toward the sea.

Alone, he looked around the littered bedroom. Dirty towels, magazines, and food cartons were strewn about. A suitcase stood open in a corner. A temporary room, as if the occupant lived most of his days somewhere else. He did—on the beach, in his car, in the taverns, and in the rooms of wandering girls.

43

Sobers had seen rooms like it before, in all the transient beach communities from coast to coast where nameless drifters polished their cars all day and dreamed of where they were going and who they would be. Temporary rooms for temporary people who spent their lives just passing through.

He began to search.

6

Roy Butler sat in his maroon Fiat sportscar in the shade of some palm trees in front of the hotel across the road from the Miramar Beach houses. He smoked and watched his house.

Blond and tanned, he was dapper in a blue blazer and pale blue slacks, but his blue shirt was dirty and wrinkled, and his quick eyes were nervous. He smoked until he saw Lois walked across the beach toward the sea.

He got out quickly, dropped his cigarette, looked all around, and then crossed the road to his house and went in the rear door. He hurried through the kitchen into the living room and stood there for a time, furtive and listening. Then he started for the stairs.

The back door opened and closed again. Butler whirled.

"What the hell do *you* want?" he snarled.

Peter Cole stood in the doorway from the kitchen. "Where's Gloria?"

Butler turned away. "Get out of here."

"Tell me where you took her!"

Peter Cole's fists clenched. Butler looked back.

"Don't threaten me, Cole. Proper and polite, that's you."

"What have you done to her? What did you want with her? She's not your kind. Where is she, Butler?"

"I don't know."

"She went away with you!"

"She went off on her own later. To hell with her."

"Alone?" Peter Cole said. "When? Where?"

"I don't know where. Some trouble about her old man." Butler was injured, a bruised ego. "First damned day!"

"Mr. . . . Forbes. He killed himself. Last night."

"Yeh," Roy Butler said. "Maybe I would have if I was married to Doris, and not just because of Russell Taylor."

"Dr. Taylor? You're a liar!"

Butler laughed without humor. "Why shouldn't your good doctor take what's offered? Listen to what he teaches a little closer. Never turn down an opportunity to get ahead."

"Dr. Taylor teaches that you *work* to get ahead."

"But it's the 'get ahead' that counts."

"Not your way!"

"What other way is there for me, sonny? A school-dropout who was going to just dazzle Hollywood. I ended up with no training, no connections, and no Dr. Taylor to give me a boost. I was stupid, but here I am, and I'm not going to fade away quietly. Accept being nothing? No. If you want what this world has to give, you grab."

"Peddling used cars and living off women?" Cole sneered.

"It beats a desk."

Peter Cole glared at Butler. "How do I know Gloria isn't still with you?"

"Because I say so," Butler snapped. "Maybe she went to you, eh? You'd do anything for her. Where were you last night?"

"Not with Gloria! And not with Mr. Forbes!"

"That makes two of us. Now beat it, I'm in a hurry."

Peter Cole hesitated, his whole body tense as if he wanted to jump at Roy Butler. Then he turned and walked out.

*

Up in the bedroom, Paul Sobers listened. He heard Peter Cole walk away, heard the door close. He went down softly.

Roy Butler stood in the living room, not moving. Sobers saw the shine on his dark, handsome face. He was sweating. As Sobers watched, Butler took out a cigarette, lit it.

"Hello, Butler," Paul Sobers said.

Roy Butler turned so fast he nearly fell over.

"Who the hell are you? What were you doing—?"

"Paul Sobers. You should know the name, right?"

"Sobers?" Butler's whole face changed, softened. An almost sad expression. "Susan's old man? Hey, I'm sorry. She was a hell of a woman. Not a goddamned kid."

Paul Sobers fought the urge to leap at Butler, to hit that incredible face. To hit . . . and hit . . . and hit . . . and . . .

"A woman," Sobers said. "Killed in a stupid robbery."

"If only I'd—" Butler stopped.

"If you'd what, Butler?"

"Okay. If I'd been with her, she wouldn't have worked."

"Who were you with? Gloria Forbes?"

"Not that night."

"Where is Gloria Forbes?"

"Who knows? I haven't seen her in almost a week."

47

"Where were you that week?"

Butler crushed out his cigarette. "I was down in Los Angeles looking for Gloria, okay? I never found her."

"Why look in Los Angeles?"

"That's where we were going, to friends of mine. I waited there, but she never showed. She was pretty upset . . . about her old man . . . something she'd found out."

Butler's voice had become smooth, sincere. A born con man, but behind the bold front he was as nervous as a stray cat in a strange city. A handsome charmer who hungered for high-living and found women easy to get, but probably not money. And money would be the only real necessity he knew, his only standard of worth, and as the years passed the face and charm would fade and the money wouldn't come any easier. Was this what Susan had wanted, searched for, preferred to him, Sobers?

"Something you told her, Butler?" he said. "Something important you had to tell her?"

"Hell, no!" The handsome face was suddenly haggard.

"What did you have to tell her?"

"Hey, I don't have to—!"

"About her mother and Russell Taylor, maybe?"

"Everyone knew about that."

"Your sister didn't, or doesn't believe it."

"Lois'd be the last—" Butler blinked. "You talked to Lois? When? What did she tell you?"

"Is there something she could tell—"

The pressure can appeared in Butler's hand. Spray hit Sobers squarely in the eyes. The pain was shattering! He groped toward Butler. A fist hit him in the face . . . in the stomach . . .

*

At the entrance to the Miramar Hotel, Jack Tracy sat with his stumps out in front of him, his pencils spread around. Sometimes the bartender brought him out a beer, and he liked to watch the beach houses across the road. A lot went on in those houses, and a man needed some fun.

He saw Paul Sobers go into Roy Butler's place, and then saw Butler slip in with Peter Cole right behind him. Cole came out, and now Butler ran out and jumped into his Fiat. Paul Sobers didn't come out.

Tracy crossed the beach road with his slow drag-clump. He reached the house, and clumped slowly into the living room. Paul Sobers lay on the floor, both hands over his eyes, his face gray and his teeth grinding in the silence of distant beach voices.

"Sobers?" Tracy said.

Paul Sobers said, "Shut up!"

"Okay," Tracy said.

Sobers said, "God damn!"

"Sure," Tracy said. "Cigarette?"

Sobers took the cigarette. His other hand still covered his eyes.

"I got a stand at the hotel," Tracy said. "Saw Butler come runnin' out 'n drive off, so I decided to come take a look."

"He drove off alone? No one in the car?"

"Far as I could see," Tracy said. "I read in the paper about that Forbes. Suicide, huh?"

"So they tell me."

"Yeh," Tracy said. "You talk to the daughter?"

"She seems to be missing."

"Yeh?" Tracy said again. "I could keep my eyes open. Who notices a cripple? Business is slow, I got time."

What had Roy Butler said? *You get ahead any way you can.* Jack Tracy had more right than most. Sobers reached into his pocket, squinted at a bill. It was a ten. He gave it to Tracy.

"On account," Tracy said. "I look for Gloria Forbes?"

"And Roy Butler."

"Butler oughta be easy. Maids 'n waitresses remember a face like that, 'n he gotta be a big show. The girl, I don' know. She don't walk my streets."

"Maybe she does now," Paul Sobers said. He stood up, his eyes still almost closed against the pain, red and tearing. He went into the bathroom, tried to wash out the eyes. It helped a little, not much. Only time would.

"First," Sobers said to Jack Tracy, "you better drive to town with me. I'll be right back."

*

Lois Butler sat on the sand in her white bikini.

"Paul! What happened to your face?"

"Does Roy always carry a can of Mace with him?"

"Roy?" She looked toward the house. "He's at—?"

"He's gone. I guess he was in a hurry."

Lois looked away out to sea. "He's never been very brave, afraid of damage to his face. That face ruined him, Paul. It made him think success would always be as easy as it had been in high school. He dropped out, went to conquer Hollywood. No talent and no discipline. All he did was play and rot."

"Peter Cole seems convinced that Gloria Forbes isn't Roy's type at all."

She took a cigarette from her pack, lit it. "Roy does usually chase older women. They admire him more."

"Yet he made a big play for Gloria Forbes."

"I don't know if it was big or small."

Sobers turned to leave.

"Paul" Lois Butler said. "Call me?"

"Sure," he said.

*

In the rented Impala, Paul Sobers drove slowly, peering ahead through slitted eyes. Jack Tracy sat beside him, guiding.

"Okay, go ahead," Tracy said. He offered Sobers another cigarette. Paul Sobers shook his head, and Tracy lit one for himself. "This Henry Forbes, he knew Susan?"

"Only at Ruston's clinic—or so he said."

"The rich," Jack Tracy said, bitter. "What the hell problems did he have bad enough for suicide?"

"Problems are relative, Jack," Sobers said.

"You got a red light," Tracy instructed. "Are they happy to be way out in front? Rich people? No, they're jumpy all the time 'cause they got to stay out front. They're scared if they don't grab for more they'll lose what they got."

"It's hard all over," Sobers said. His eyes throbbed.

"Green, go straight on," Tracy said. "The rich ain't the worst, though. That's the nice, solid folks who works all their lives at what they never much wanted to and still believes all the same things the rich do. They'll die fightin' for what they ain't never gonna have."

"You don't do that, Jack?" Sobers said, talked out the pain.

"I float. Got nothin', don't want nothin'." The legless man watched the traffic. "When I lost the legs I went down all the way. Then somethin' happened. I was out of it, the whole race, so I relaxed. Maybe losin' the legs made me see clear."

He guided Sobers in a left turn. "I move around sellin' the pencils. Go by bus, live in hotels. Summers back east, winters out here. Ask nobody to buy, cops never bother me, 'n I clear maybe twenty-five a day. Only expenses are the pencils, a room, 'n half-soles for my 'shoes' every year. Made the shoes myself. Artificial legs made my stumps hurt. It'd be okay if it was just one leg, I could favor the wooden leg when it got sore. With two you can't rest 'em."

"You don't get lonely?"

"Sometimes. I watch people. I go places. I read a lot."

"How'd you lose the legs?"

"In a blizzard. They froze on me."

They reached Sobers' motel, and he called a taxi to take Jack Tracy to his room at the Carrillo Hotel. Tracy grinned back as he walked his slow drag-clump to the waiting cab. A tough little figure in the winter sun.

7

At the elegant, inlaid writing desk in the book-lined library of the big house on Mission Ridge, Doris Forbes worked with documents strewn all around her. In an open-necked green shirt and tight green slacks that showed off her trim figure, her blonde hair tied back, she added columns of figures and drank a martini. The housekeeper came in.

"Peter Cole to see you."

Doris Forbes scowled, then nodded, and the housekeeper left. Doris Forbes drank, drummed her slender fingers on the desk, and then turned to Peter Cole with a smile as he came into the room.

"Hello, Peter. I'm afraid I haven't heard from her."

"I just talked to Butler."

"Roy? Then Gloria—?"

"He was alone," Peter Cole said. "He says that Gloria left him the first day she was gone. Went off alone."

"Alone?" Doris Forbes said. She drank her martini. "Well, that's good, at least. But where in heavens is she?"

"Butler said she talked about some trouble, Mrs. Forbes. Some trouble about Mr. Forbes."

"About Henry?"

"What was it? Could she have come back and—?"

"Don't be stupid, Peter!"

"Okay," Peter Cole said. "But Mr. Forbes is dead! He shot himself. Maybe whatever the trouble was Gloria talked to Butler about is what made him—"

"No, Peter. Forget that, you understand? Henry didn't kill himself, and if Gloria had some problem with Henry it might have made her run off, but that's all."

Peter Cole stood there in the library for a moment. Then he nodded.

"Yes, ma'am," he said. "If . . . when . . ."

"I'll tell you the moment she returns, Peter."

The youth walked out. Doris Forbes sat there unmoving. Then she picked up her martini, took a slow drink.

*

In his motel room, Paul Sobers lay on the bed with the shades drawn. He had washed his eyes twice more, slept for an hour or so, and the pain had ebbed to a dull ache.

The ache blended in the dim afternoon room with the ache for Susan. A year of aching, waiting for her. Now she was dead. How long could he ache? What was he doing? Playing at detective for what? He'd been hit, half-blinded, and for what? She was gone, and she'd been gone from him long before that. To find a cheap drifter like Roy Butler. Gone to Roy Butler and to what else? Did he really want to know? She was dead; maybe the rest was better left unknown. She'd died in a robbery. The wrong place at the wrong time. Let it rest there.

He reached for a cigarette, feeling a weight lift from him. Beckett was right, go home, Sobers. He was no detect . . . He looked at the cigarette package in his hands. A matchbook had been pushed under the outer cellophane. He never did that, and they weren't his brand. He

54

looked at the matchbook—Redwood Motel, Nogales, Marin.

Jack Tracy's pack? No, Tracy had smoked in the car. Lois Butler had had her cigarettes on the beach.

Peter Cole? No, Cole hadn't smoked anytime, probably didn't smoke. But Roy Butler had smoked. Butler who claimed he'd been in Los Angeles the whole last week without Gloria Forbes.

Sobers got up, washed his eyes again, and went out.

*

Otto Genseric, president and chairman of Calixco Petroleum, was a medium-sized, silver-haired man in his early seventies. A well-fed man, pink-faced and barbered, but not soft.

"If Henry Forbes shot himself, it wasn't over anything at Calixco," Genseric said.

He sat across a desk from Lee Beckett in the county prosecutor's office. Prosecutor Tucker had asked him to come to the office, and Genseric wasn't too pleased to be turned over to a subordinate. His manner was weighty, his voice curt. His eyes showed annoyance. His silver hair was arranged and his suit was expensive, but he wore high-heeled western boots, and his hands were rough. A combination of corporate power and rugged individualism, and he was still president of Calixco at over seventy because he owned Calixco.

"Was he murdered over anything at Calixco?" Beckett said.

"Murdered? Ridiculous!"

"He was either shot, or he shot himself, Mr. Genseric."

"I meant that it's ridiculous to even consider that anything in his work could have been a motive for either," Otto Genseric said testily. "Unless you think he could

55

have been shot just because he worked for Calixco. A few years ago, when the bird-lovers were after our blood, I'd have said, yes, look for some crazy ecologist. But that has all calmed down, eh? Reformers never last long."

"You can give us no reason for suicide or murder?"

"None," Genseric said.

"He was happy in his work? No problems?"

"Henry was never the happiest of men. Over-sensitive and moody, tended to work too hard. He could have had a position at Calixco with much less travel, but he seemed to prefer the work with a lot of travel."

"A rocky home life?"

"Perhaps less than what he wanted," Genseric said.

"But all he wanted at work?"

"Yes, I really think so. Henry wasn't an ambitious man. I often—" Genseric looked at the door.

The door opened and Paul Sobers came in. He saw Genseric, nodded to Lee Beckett, lit a cigarette, and stood quietly in a corner. Beckett watched him for a moment.

"Paul Sobers, Mr. Otto Genseric," Beckett said. "Sobers is connected to the case, Mr. Genseric. Sobers, Mr. Genseric is the president of Calixco Petroleum, Henry Forbes's company." Beckett nodded to Genseric. "All right, Henry Forbes wasn't ambitious. Just what was his job with you?"

"Job?" The plebian word pained Otto Genseric. "He was a senior lawyer specializing in government affairs, regulations."

"Government affairs can be touchy for an oil company," Beckett said. "Maybe there was some business problem you didn't know about."

Otto Genseric snorted, the idea was preposterous.

"He was going on a business trip for you?"

"No, a personal trip. He asked for a month off."

"You know where he was going?"

"I'm sorry, I don't." Genseric looked at his watch. "I—"

Paul Sobers said, "He was out of town for a day recently. Was that on Calixco business, Mr. Genseric?"

"I don't know," Genseric said impatiently. "Henry didn't consult with me on every routine matter."

"We may have to look into his work," Beckett said. "I expect you'd cooperate, Mr. Genseric."

"Would I? My business isn't your affair, Beckett."

"Tucker was elected to do a job."

Beckett smiled. So did Otto Genseric. They both knew that Genseric hadn't elected Prosecutor Tucker. Opposite sides.

"Was Henry Forbes just an employee?" Paul Sobers asked. "Or perhaps a partner, an associate?"

"A high-level employee, but that was all."

"Forbes was a long way from rich, Sobers," Beckett said. "You wanted to know what he had. The Mission Ridge house and its twenty-odd acres are worth maybe two hundred fifty thousand dollars now; the beach house another hundred thousand. His salary, and that's it. No stocks, no big money, and the houses weren't even Forbes's. They belong to Doris Forbes. She had them before she married Forbes."

Genseric said, "Henry used to joke about his rich marriage. The poor California boy who worked hard and made good."

"Rich?" Sobers said. "Beckett just told us—"

"Henry was being ironic, Mr. Sobers," Otto Genseric said. He looked at his watch again and stood. "Keep me informed, Beckett, and give my best to Charley Tucker."

Genseric left, and Paul Sobers sat down. He told Beckett about meeting Roy Butler and what Butler had said —and about the Mace attack.

"Gloria Forbes went off alone?" Beckett said.

"That's what he says, but he sure didn't want me around. If he's here today, he could have been here last night."

"We'll pick him up," Beckett said. "Sobers, can we stop you before you really get hurt? You've been Maced, slugged, and you haven't found a damn thing."

"I found that big man who jumped me. His name's Kapek, he's an ex-con. He says he lent the book of poems to Gloria, was just getting it back. Says he was drunk last night and doesn't even remember attacking me."

"We found him too. You see? He's been in town a month, on vacation. He's from New York, has a rented car, and he may be an ex-con but he's not on any current 'wanted' list in New York or Sacramento. Two bartenders confirm that he was drinking last night in West Side bars. His only connection we can find is to Gloria—he lent her a book." Beckett shook his head. "Look, hang around if you have to, we've got a nice city. But play golf, go swimming."

"I don't like golf," Sobers said. He stood up. "I wonder where Henry Forbes was going for a month?"

"Does it matter?" Beckett said. "He didn't go."

*

Sobers closed the door of his motel room. Doris Forbes sat on the bed.

"The manager let me in," she said. "I told him I was your secretary from New York."

"You know your way around motels."

She didn't react. Composed, even cool. Sobers sat down.

"I suppose I did sound fairly awful last night," she said. "So many men, so many motels. But not *that* many men, really, and I'm not here to add you to the list."

"That's too bad," Sobers said.

58

Her smile was direct and unembarrassed.

"Have I made a conquest, Paul? A friend?"

Naked, next to Lois Butler she would look almost like a boy, but she had much more. Brittle and arranged when he'd met her, she seemed open and gentle now, soft, and he felt that underneath she always had been. The kind of woman you want to be with.

"Have you had lunch?" he asked.

"No." She took a breath. "Paul, I haven't told—"

"Let's talk over some food."

He drove to a restaurant he'd seen high on a cliff above the sea. Few people were eating so late in the afternoon. The ocean rolled below the cliff, and seagulls wheeled outside. He ordered abalone. She had only a crabmeat salad.

"I haven't been here for years," she said. "Russ thinks it too expensive for college business, and Henry. . . ." She let her eyes follow a great brown pelican skim the waves far out. "Henry always said I wouldn't let him love me the way he wanted, and he never could love me the way I wanted."

"Always?" Sobers said. "Then it's not much of a reason for suicide now. Or do you still think it wasn't suicide?"

"I . . . I don't know. I don't think he did, but—"

The waiter came with their lunch. Doris Forbes waited with her eyes down until the waiter had gone. Then she looked up.

"Gloria isn't Henry's daughter, Paul. Henry was my second husband." She began to toy with her crabmeat. "My first husband was a boy from San Vicente, but I didn't meet him here, and we never lived here. We met in San Francisco in 1955, in North Beach. I don't expect you can imagine me in North Beach among the beatniks back then, but I was. Twenty-one, born in genteel poverty, working in a bookstore when I met Johnny."

"Johnny?" Sobers put down his fork.

She nodded. "He came from an old family here, well-off but not rich. His father had the houses, a small income, and a lot of contacts ready to give Johnny a career. But Johnny was a poet, so he went up to North Beach, and we got married. Gloria was born in 1956, and we moved to an art colony in Marin. Not a commune, that wasn't the fashion yet, but an old bohemian had land on a mountain and sold plots on long term without interest to any artist who'd build his own home. We did."

She watched the pelican dive into the sea far out. "For a time we were happy. Then . . . Perhaps it was my fault, I never should have tried that life. Or perhaps it was Johnny; perhaps he never could have adjusted to marriage, a family. Probably it was both of us. I had a child, I came to hate that half-gypsy life, pushed him to come here and live with his father. He could write here, I'd get a job, we'd have security. He hated the idea. He began to drink. We shut each other out, grew apart. Something had to happen."

"John Glavin," Sobers said. "Gloria had his book of poems. What did happen back then, Doris?"

At sea, the pelican flew up. Clumsy on the water, it was magnificent in the air. "Johnny was away one week; I went to a man. The sordid old story, Johnny found us. He was drunk, there was a terrible fight, the man died. Johnny was a college boxer. They charged him with murder. His father got a lawyer, and they let him plead guilty to manslaughter. Prison—for one-to-twenty-five years!

"I brought Gloria to live with Johnny's father. I nursed the old man, and when he died in 1962 he left all he had to us. In 1963 I divorced Johnny—he could have been in prison twenty more years! I married Henry. In 1965 we heard Johnny had been released. But he never came near us, and in 1966 we were told he was dead in Wyoming. We sent money to bury him properly."

She stirred at her salad. "Three weeks ago, Gloria showed me the poem from the book. I knew it. Johnny had written it in 1957. Gloria was agitated, upset."

"She hadn't known Glavin was her father? Someone told her?"

"No, she knew. We never hid Johnny. But we had hidden what really happened. We'd told her that he died in 1959."

"The true story upset her? Prison? The killing?"

"She said I'd cheated her. I didn't know how much she knew, so I told her the whole truth, but I'm not sure she believed me. When Peter told me that Roy Butler was back and that Gloria had gone off alone somewhere—"

"You think she went up to Marin County."

She nodded. "And it's been so . . . long."

"Do you know a man named Frank Kapek? A big, bearded man?"

"No. Is he someone important to all this?"

"I don't know," Sobers said. "Did you tell Henry about it all?"

"No. He loved Gloria. He'd have been frantic."

"I think he knew—and he was." He told her about the fight Janine McGrath had heard on the beach. "Doris, Roy Butler may have been in Marin, not Los Angeles. You better tell the police."

"No, Paul!" She was pale. "If Gloria—"

"You want me to go up there?"

"Would you, Paul?"

"I guess I'm in deep enough already," he said.

Doris leaned across the table, kissed him.

*

At the garden apartments where Janine McGrath and Frank Kapek lived, Sobers found the manager and asked for Kapek.

"I'm afraid he's gone," the manager said. "Left us today. No forwarding address. These short-renters never leave one."

Sobers drove on to the airport.

8

It was dark when Paul Sobers landed in San Francisco. He rented a car. A winter fog hid the bay as he drove across the Golden Gate Bridge into Marin County.

The lights in the neat houses of suburban San Francisco were soft and hazy through the fog. He drove steadily north on Highway 101 through the art colonies of Sausalito, the county seat of San Rafael, and left the fog behind before he reached Novato. There he turned on a county road into the hills.

It was rough country, cold and clear on the January night. Compared to the grape valleys just east in Sonoma, it was poor, dry land, with ragged farmhouses dotting the slopes.

Nogales was a one-street town with stores, two saloons, a movie house, and the mountains looming around it. He pulled into the only motel, the Redwood Motel. A quick-eyed old man in corduroy pants and boots looked up behind the desk. Sobers showed him the picture he had of Gloria Forbes.

"Gloria Forbes," he said. "Has she been here?"

"Well, seems kind of familiar." The old man looked at

the picture, then at Sobers. "What was the name?"

"Gloria Forbes. Maybe a week ago she—"

The old man went into a small office, rummaged around out of sight. After a time, he came back carrying a register.

"No Gloria Forbes. When you say she was here?"

"Anywhere from eight days ago to today," Sobers said.

The old man studied the ledger. "Any idea what name she was maybe using?"

"No," Sobers said. "She might not have been alone."

"Like that?" The old man went down the pages with his finger. "She from San Francisco. Somewhere near?"

"From San Vicente."

"That far, eh? She in trouble?"

Sobers watched the old man move his eyes slowly over each page. All at once he realized that the old man wasn't really reading the names in the register. He was stalling.

"Where is she," Sobers said. "You know, don't you?"

His pistol was in his belt, but the old man moved faster. The old man had the advantage; he'd been prepared to move. The sawed-off shotgun appeared in his hands from under the desk.

"Just stay quiet, you won't get hurt," the old man said.

"What have you done—?"

The old man cocked the shotgun.

"Just relax, mister. It won't be too long."

It wasn't. The old man had to have made a telephone call while he was in the office. Sobers heard the car stop outside. Two men came in behind him. A hand took the gun from his belt.

*

The president's house at Newmont College was a two-story brown frame set among trees with a porch around three sides. Dr. Russell Taylor stood in the living room with his back to the fire in the fireplace. The nights were cold in Buena Costa County in winter.

"You sent that Sobers up to Marin? Was that wise?" Doris Forbes sat on a deep old couch.

"We have to find Gloria, Russ," she said.

Dr. Martin Ruston leaned back in an easy chair near the fire. The stout physician was as blunt and business-like as usual.

"And we have to find her soon," he said.

"That Sobers is something of a bulldog," Russell Taylor said. "If she's up there, he'll find her. Only he could be something of a problem later."

"Then we'll handle him," Ruston snapped. "He simply doesn't want to accept the truth about his wife. A simple robbery."

"Yes," Taylor said. He seemed to think. "You're guessing that Gloria's gone up to Marin after the shadow of your first husband, Doris?"

"I think so," Doris Forbes said.

Ruston snorted. "An example of why it's always best to tell all the truth you can. Evasion never pays."

"Don't tell me what I could and couldn't tell Gloria, Martin!"

"You've dug yourself a mess by not telling her!"

Taylor said, "Or someone dug us a mess. Roy Butler, I suppose."

"Or that person you said Sobers mentioned," Ruston said. "Frank Kapek, was it? Who the devil is he?"

"I have no idea," Doris Forbes said.

"Well," Ruston said, "at least you can bury Henry tomorrow. The police have released the body."

"We'll wait a few more days," Doris Forbes said. "Gloria would want to be here."

"Yes," Russell Taylor said. "I wonder if someone did murder Henry? If so, who?"

Only the fire broke the silence of the room.

*

"Yes," Sobers said. "It's Gloria Forbes."

The hospital was in San Rafael. The sheriff's deputies who had taken his pistol at the Redwood Motel drove him there in his own car. A lieutenant named Kincaid met him at the hospital. Kincaid was an older man with a weathered face. Together they looked down at the girl silent in the bed.

"She was shot twice at that motel in Nogales," Lieutenant Kincaid said. "Shoulder, chest, and she had a concussion. That's all we knew. She's been unconscious or delirious. No luggage, no handbag, no identification, and she didn't fit any missing persons tracer."

"She wasn't reported missing," Sobers said.

They left the dim room, and Sobers waited in the glare of the corridor while Kincaid went to have Doris Forbes notified. Kincaid lit a thin cigar when he returned.

"She registered alone?" Sobers asked.

"Yes and no. She arrived alone, but signed Mr. and Mrs. Henry Glavin and said her husband was joining her. She didn't have a car, was dropped at the Redwood. The clerk heard her talking to a man later in her unit, figured it was the husband. We haven't found any husband. The San Francisco address she gave was phony. The other guests all check out clean."

"No one saw this 'husband'?"

"Nope."

"When did it happen? What day?"

"The eleventh. She checked in about three P.M. on the tenth, about one A.M. the shots woke up the clerk. We get hunters up here in winter, so the clerk thought it was some hunter too close to town. Only then he heard a lot of noise—window smashing, door slamming, loud action, and some voices. He got up when he heard a car drive off. By the time he got to her unit, the whole motel was up and yelling. He called us, we brought her here, waited for her to tell us who she was, or for someone to show up and tell us."

"No clues? What kind of gun was it?"

"A .32-caliber pistol, we didn't find it. No clues."

"Did anyone hear her say anything? About why she came?"

"She asked about a mountain colony out that way, but she didn't go anywhere, just stayed in her room. No one at the colony recognized her description. You going to wait here?"

Sobers nodded, and Kincaid walked away along the bright corridor. A deputy remained on guard in front of Gloria Forbes's hospital room. Sobers smoked. Outside, the small city grew quiet as the hours passed. A rural city, dark and silent in the late night, on a different planet from San Francisco or Los Angeles. Sobers went on waiting, and thinking of Susan who hadn't had the luck to need a hospital room.

Doris Forbes arrived near one A.M. A doctor took her into the room. She barely glanced at Paul Sobers. He waited, and she came out after ten minutes. Her face was drained, drawn, but she wasn't shaking. Even calm, a strength in her eyes, as if now she had something she could do.

"How is she?" Sobers asked.

"The doctors say she should live. Should!"

Her voice was flat, almost distant, as if the shock of seeing Gloria lying shot in a hospital bed had made her forget her own small needs. Isolated in a sudden present. A crisis can do that, suspend time in the instant.

"Has she said anything at all?" Sobers asked.

"No."

"The police have no leads. No idea who or why."

"Who?" Doris said. "I have to make a call."

She went along the corridor. A doctor came, and went into Gloria's room. Sobers followed him in, waited while the doctor examined the silent girl. He could see the thick bandages on her chest and shoulder under the covers.

"Will she be okay?" Sobers asked.

The doctor nodded. "She should recover rapidly now. The wounds aren't too serious—mostly shock and loss of blood."

"Can she talk?"

"No," the doctor said. He walked out of the room.

Sobers moved closer to the bed. In person, Gloria Forbes's long Celtic face was prettier, more open and sensitive. He saw now that she didn't look like Forbes and not much like Doris, but maybe that was only because he knew who her father had been. Her dark hair had red tinges, and her body curved long under the covers. She breathed quietly, but as Sobers watched she began to move, restless. She moaned, mumbled:

". . . alive . . . on the moon . . . call my name. . . ."

Sobers recognized the words of John Glavin's poem.

". . . dead . . . they made him dead . . . they . . ."

He leaned closer, but the girl's voice trailed off, and a nurse came in and ordered him out. In the corridor, Doris Forbes stood alone. She tried to smile.

"You've been a great help, Paul. Not many men would have done so much for a stranger."

"I have my own reasons, too," he said.

"Yes. We've both lost—" She suddenly held to the wall. Her lips smiled, but her eyes were battered. "I seem to feel a bit weak. I suppose I need rest, but I can't leave Gloria."

68

"What can you do?" Sobers said. "There're sure to be some motels close by where you could be called fast."

"We will need our strength tomorrow. But I'll go only if you do too."

The nurse on duty had the number of the nearest motel; the hospital had a fixed arrangement to notify relatives if they were needed. Sobers steadied Doris down in the elevator and across the street to the motel. They registered. He took both keys and held her arm as they walked to their units in the cold late night hours. He unlocked her door, helped her inside, and started to go to find his unit.

"No," she said. She closed her door, stood close to him with her face turned up. "Stay, Paul."

Perhaps it was that they had each lost someone, had both had someone shot. A sense of mortality and need.

Her mouth moved against his, her body clung to his like something warm and hungry. Starved. Slim and tight in his arms like thin steel, straining, and yet somehow as soft as the touch of velvet. He carried her to the large bed.

There was no struggle. Neither of them resisted. For Sobers it had been a long time. Somehow, he couldn't while Susan was still his, somewhere. But Susan was gone . . .

Naked on the bed in the dark room. He didn't know how long it had been for her, but there were no barriers, no words. Only the sound of their bodies moving together like velvet and steel, supple and insistent . . .

He lit two cigarettes, gave her one. She lay on her back, a white shape with dark shadows and a glint of eyes.

"Our mountain colony wasn't far from here," she said. "We could still have been there if I'd been a different woman. If he hadn't married me, Johnny might have been a great poet."

"He wouldn't," Sobers said. "No one destroys a man, he destroys himself. He'd have found another way."

"A comforting idea, anyway." She lay there silent. Then her hand touched Sobers. "He must have been out of his mind after all, Paul. Sick inside."

"He?" Sobers said.

"Henry. We can't hide from it now, can we? I suppose he wanted to shoot Butler. He came up here after them, tried to kill Roy, and shot Gloria. He must have thought he'd killed her. That's why he killed himself. Poor Henry."

"You think Henry killed himself after all?"

"What else is there to think?"

They lay there silent, each with private thoughts, and when she fell asleep, Sobers got up and went to his own room.

He wanted to be alone now, and, alone, he lay awake for a long time in the cold mountain night. If Forbes had shot Gloria and himself, who had shot Susan?

*

Sobers opened his eyes to the crisp sunlight of the northern California winter. His watch read nine A.M. He jumped up, shaved, showered, and went to call Doris.

There was no answer at her room. He tried the door. It was open! Inside, the room was empty. He went to the office.

"Mrs. Forbes?" the clerk said. "Yes, she checked out about seven A.M. Her doctors came for her."

"Doctors?"

"Yes, sir, there were two doctors who came for her."

Sobers went to the hospital. The deputy was gone from the door of Gloria Forbes's room.

"We released Miss Forbes this morning," the head nurse told him, "to her mother and a Dr. Ruston from

San Vincente. The police and our staff okayed it, she went in an ambulance to the airport."

Sobers found Lieutenant Kincaid at the sheriff's office in downtown San Rafael.

"You let Mrs. Forbes take Gloria home?"

"No reason to keep her," Kincaid said. "She was able to tell us some of it this morning. Seems she was at the Redwood with a guy named Roy Butler. They were having a drink, heard someone behind the unit. Butler must have been nervous. He jumped up, turned off the lights, and someone fired four shots through the window. The girl was hit, and that's all she knows."

"Why was she up here with Butler in the first place?"

"She passed out again before I could ask her that. We'll go on looking, but this Butler looks like the key. I passed it all on to Sheriff Hoag down in San Vicente."

"Did Doris Forbes tell you what she thinks happened?"

Kincaid shook his head. "Didn't talk to her."

"You didn't see her this morning? I thought you said—"

"Saw a guy named Taylor, and a Dr. Ruston from San Vicente. They had the hospital release, said Mrs. Forbes had collapsed, was in the ambulance with the girl."

Sobers said, "Can I have my gun? I've got a New York permit."

"That's no good here, Sobers, but I'll pass it this time. Only you better not carry it anymore, okay?"

Sobers left. Would Doris have left without a word to him? After last night? Or was that just male ego?

He drove down toward San Francisco in the rented car. At a roadside tavern, he stopped and called Doris in San Vicente. There was no answer at the Forbes house. Where was she?

Sobers sent a telegram to Jack Tracy. He told the

crippled pencil-seller to check at the Ruston Clinic, and gave the time of the flight he could get out of San Francisco.

Then he drove on south.

9

Jack Tracy sat in the entrance to the Ruston Clinic, his pencils and upturned hat in front of him. He collected little from patients going in, and nothing from the doctors, but the patients coming out were generous.

"Thank you, sir . . . Bless you, ma'am . . ."

He saw nothing of Doris or Gloria Forbes, but Russell Taylor came out alone about ten o'clock, the sheriff visited briefly, and Peter Cole hurried inside just before eleven. Cole came out almost at once.

"How are they, son? The girl and her mother?" Tracy asked, his voice humble. "They was always nice to me."

"I didn't see them," Peter Cole said. He was angry.

When the youth had gone, Tracy clumped his slow way inside with his hat in his hands, and asked to see Doris Forbes.

"I'm a friend," he said, "and I got 'n important message from the guy found Gloria for her. Paul Sobers."

"I'm sorry," the receptionist said. "Mrs. Forbes is under sedation. Absolutely no visitors."

Tracy returned to selling his pencils. The maroon Fiat sportscar drove into the parking lot at about eleven-thirty. No one got out. Dr. Martin Ruston strode past the legless old man without looking at him, got into the Fiat, and the car drove away with a screech of tires.

Tracy waited until past twelve-thirty. The Fiat didn't return.

*

The jet from San Francisco landed in San Vicente at one. Paul Sobers saw Jack Tracy waiting at the Impala.

"You found the girl up in Marin?" Tracy said. "What happened up there?"

Sobers told him everything Gloria had said.

"Who'd want to shoot the girl?"

"Not Gloria, Roy Butler," Sobers said. "They worked it out that Henry Forbes tried to kill Butler, hit Gloria by mistake. He thought he'd killed her, and that's why he shot himself."

Sobers started the car almost violently and drove out of the airport parking lot. He drove in silence to the freeway entrance and merged into the traffic going south. Jack Tracy watched him as they drove.

"You don't figure it happened like that?" Tracy said.

"It leaves some loose ends."

"Like your wife?" Tracy said. "You ever think maybe you just gotta know she died in some big, crooked mess? Got trapped in some other folks trouble? Not just because she was alone 'n workin'? Because she wasn't with you no more?"

"I've thought about that!" Sobers said savagely. "I think about it all the time! Do I want to think she was murdered in some devious plot so I can't blame myself? She didn't die just because she had to leave me? But there are other loose strings, too. Frank Kapek, for instance, and John Glavin's poems, and why Gloria and Butler went up to Marin. If they were just running off together, why to Marin? I want to talk to Butler."

"Maybe you should talk to that Doc Ruston, then," Tracy said. "I saw Butler's Fiat in the clinic parkin' lot. Ruston got in and took a ride."

"Ruston? With Roy Butler?"

"I didn't see Butler, but it was his car."

"What about Doris Forbes? Did you locate her? See her?"

"She's at Ruston's clinic with the girl. I tried to see her, no dice. That Peter Cole tried to get in too, 'n they shooed him off. Looks like someone don't want people to talk to her or the girl."

"You mean they're holding her like a prisoner?"

"Sure looks a lot like that to me," Tracy said.

Sobers drove in silence for a time, pulling out to roar past slower moving cars as the freeway circled the city toward the suburb of Santecito.

"I'll see her," he said. "And I'll find out about Ruston and Roy Butler."

*

In the thickly wooded suburb of Santecito, the Ruston Clinic was two yellow brick buildings hidden among trees. A two-story main building and hospital, and the outpatient and laboratory center where Susan had died. Sobers dropped Jack Tracy at his Miramar Hotel stand before driving on to the clinic.

In the main building, Sobers gave his name and asked for Dr. Ruston. The receptionist looked at him curiously as she operated her intercom. She'd probably known Susan, but she said nothing and sent him along the green corridors to Ruston's office. He went in without knocking.

Ruston was at his desk, didn't look up as Sobers came in. In a suit and tie instead of a white coat, he worked on papers.

"What do you want, Sobers?"

His crisp voice was blunt and not very friendly.

"To see Doris Forbes. And Gloria, too, if she can talk."

"She can't," Ruston said, "and Mrs. Forbes needs complete rest, is sedated, and wants to see no one just yet."

"Doesn't want to see anyone, or isn't being allowed to see anyone?"

Ruston looked up sharply. "Get out of here, Mr. Sobers!"

"You met with Roy Butler today. Why?"

"Butler?" Ruston said. He leaned back in his chair. "That, I think, is my business. Now go away, Sobers."

"No! I demand to see—"

"Demand?" Ruston leaned forward. "You demand nothing! You're breaking the law this very minute. You're probably paranoid, yes. Now you—"

"I'm going to talk to Doris Forbes," Sobers said quietly and moved his hand toward his belt.

Ruston was up. "Help! He's got a gun! Help!"

The two burly men in white suits seemed to come from nowhere. They grabbed Sobers, held him. One had a hypodermic syringe . . .

*

Paul Sobers opened his eyes to the shadow of long, thin stripes on a whitewashed wall. He lay on a narrow cot hanging from the wall. He saw a washstand and a toilet. He had never been inside a jail before, but he knew where he was.

The first thing he did was climb onto the toilet and look out the barred window. Buena Costa County jail is on the top floor of the old brick courthouse. He saw palms and tall pines and people walking along the street in the sun below.

The second thing he did was start shouting.

"Hey! Out there! What am I doing here! Hey! Sheriff!"

Shouts that echoed along the cell block corridor, and

when he paused for breath, all along the corridor unseen voices took up the clamor. A crescendo of noise like the howling pandemonium in a dog kennel when a new dog is brought in.

A guard ran up. "Shut it off! You hear? Shut up!"

"Man want to know what he doin' here, Boss!"

"Tell the man what he doin' here, Cap'n!"

"Look, Ma, I'm innocent!"

Mocking catcalls.

"One minute, no privileges for twenty-four! I'm counting."

Silence.

"That's better." The guard laughed.

Sobers gripped the bars of his cell door.

"I want the sheriff, Lee Beckett! I want—!"

The billy club smashed against his fingers. He cursed in pain. He jumped back from the bars.

"Be nice now," the guard said.

Sobers sat in the cell. No one came.

*

They ate in a narrow mess hall with guards. The guards did nothing. It was what they could do, had the power to do.

Night, and breakfast, and lunch, and night. At the high window Sobers stood a million miles from the street below. On another planet.

*

"You wanted to talk to me, Sobers?"

Sheriff John Hoag was a stocky man with a bland face that revealed nothing.

"What am I doing in here!"

"You don't remember? About attacking Dr. Ruston? About using a gun? About your wife's murder?"

"My wife?" Sobers was scared. "I didn't—!"

"You know a lawyer?"

"Lois Butler?"

The sheriff nodded.

*

Two prisoners beat a third in the recreation hall. The guards took the victim away. Sobers shrank into the corner of his cell. He tried to think of Susan, of Doris Forbes, of Dr. Ruston. All he could think of was himself.

*

Lois Butler wore a blue dress, smelled of air and sunlight.

"Assault with a deadly weapon, illegal possession of a handgun, interference with the police, and suspicion of murder in the death of your wife. No bail because of the murder charge."

"Good God!" Sobers said.

"They don't believe the murder part, Paul, just want to teach you a lesson. Sit tight, do nothing. I'll work on it. They buried Henry Forbes two days ago. You can bury your wife. Do you want the funeral here?"

"Why not?" he said.

*

Sobers had been in jail two weeks on the day of the funeral. He walked out behind Hoag like a crab blinded by the sun.

They held a brief service in the chapel and drove to the cemetery. Lois Butler was there, and Lee Beckett. Jack Tracy's head barely rose above the coffin. Dr. Russell Taylor brought condolences from Doris Forbes. She was still in the clinic.

Susan was buried.

Sobers looked down at the mound of fresh earth, and suddenly, as if the sky had split blue above, his life would never be the same. His life would be something else, something unknown.

*

Sheriff Hoag sat behind the desk in his office. Lee Beckett leaned on a wall behind Sobers.

"You stuck your nose in and your neck out," Hoag said. "I want to make sure you never do it again."

"I just wanted to talk to Doris Forbes, and—"

Beckett said, "Gloria's still in the clinic, but she told us a couple of points. About a year ago, Doris Forbes had one of her affairs—with Roy Butler. She told Gloria to shock her out of seeing Butler. Before Gloria ran off, she told Henry Forbes she was going up to Marin with Butler. So Forbes knew where they were, and had another reason to keep Butler from Gloria—his wife's lover now chasing his daughter."

"Not his daughter."

"He raised her," Hoag said. "To him she was his."

"Why wait a week and plan a trip before suicide?"

"He hoped he hadn't killed her," Beckett said. "But when he heard nothing from Marin he thought she was dead."

"What about Frank Kapek? Why did he take John Glavin's book back after Gloria was shot?"

"He was leaving town," Hoag said. "He wanted his book."

"He knew Glavin once, gave Glavin's book to Gloria, but didn't know she was Glavin's daughter? That's coincidence!"

"You learn slow, don't you?" Sheriff Hoag said. "Still playing at detective."

Beckett said, "Say Kapek did know Gloria was Glavin's kid. So what? Kapek was in San Vicente when Gloria was shot, and in some bar when Forbes was. And it's not Kapek that bugs you, it's your wife. You never believed the robbery. Okay, and you're right. It wasn't robbery. We checked Henry Forbes's gun. It's the same gun that shot your wife."

The silence in the office pressed down like a weight.

"We picked up Roy Butler," Beckett said, "and he admitted that he *was* with your wife that night at the clinic. When she was shot he ran like a deer, never saw the killer. He believed it had been a robber until the shooting in Marin. Then he realized *he* was probably the target at the clinic, too. Forbes tried to shoot him then, killed your wife instead."

"He tried to shoot Butler twice and missed twice?"

"Better odds than missing once. He was a lousy shot," Beckett said. "Your wife meant nothing to him, but when he thought he'd killed Gloria, that broke him."

"And he shot himself," Hoag said. "Now we know."

"All you know is that the same gun shot them both!"

The sheriff reddened. "Okay, we drop the murder charge, but you're a hardhead, Sobers. The other charges stand!"

*

In his silent cell Sobers waited for his bail money from New York. Then what? Beckett was right. It was easier to believe a man missing twice at close range than missing once. The second miss helped prove the first. And what did he, Sobers, have to offer? A book of poems by a man dead eleven years, a doctor who protected his patients, and wild guesses.

If he pleaded guilty, apologized, maybe they would let him go home. To an empty apartment and to cry for Susan. He hadn't cried yet. Not when she had left him, not when she had died. He had wanted to know first why she had died. Now he knew—for nothing. His wife had died for nothing, could he cry now?

"Okay, Sobers, you've been bailed. Come on."

It was too soon for money to have come from New York, but he followed the guard without a word. When the jail door opens, you ask no questions. He was learning about a different world. There were formalities, forms, and instructions about the rules of his bail. They returned his personal effects, without his gun, and gave him the keys to his rented Impala.

The car was in the courthouse lot. It wasn't empty.

"You drive, Mr. Sobers," Gloria Forbes said.

She sat in the front seat. Her dark hair with its red tinge had been cut short. It made her sensitive Celtic face longer and older. She was pale and thin, and there was no smile in her eyes. Anger was in the young eyes, and pain. Bandages still bulked under her man's shirt and denim jacket, but the pain in her eyes was only partly physical.

"You put up my bail?" Sobers said.

"I got a bondsman, yes."

"Beckett said you were still in the clinic."

"I am," she said. "Ruston's jail. I went over the wall."

"What do you want from me, Gloria?"

"Help. I want you to help me. There's no one else."

"No," he said. "It's all over. Your father—"

"Henry Forbes wasn't my father, and it isn't over." She looked out at all the people passing beyond the lot in the warm winter sun. "They lied to me all my life, took my father away from me. But Roy told me the truth. I could have known him, my father! I could have known who he was, what he was! I could have gone to him, helped him! Maybe if I'd gone to him he—"

"They were only trying to protect you, Gloria."

"Protect *me?*" She turned to face him, her gaunt young face hard with the inflexible judgment of youth. "You don't know?"

"Know?" Sobers said.

Her laugh was like steel. "You don't know how my mother and Henry met? They met up there in Marin— where Henry Forbes was the prosecutor who sent my real father to prison!"

Sobers turned the key in the ignition, drove slowly out of the courthouse lot. He drove toward his motel.

"Roy Butler told you that?"

"Yes! My mother married the man who sent her husband to prison!"

"Your mother sent me to Marin after you," Sobers said. "She was worried, even scared. Now you want help. Help to do what? What was Doris afraid you might find in Marin? What else did Roy Butler tell you?"

A fear mixed on her young face with hope.

"You think John Glavin is alive, don't you?" Sobers said. "And you're afraid it wasn't Forbes who shot you and himself."

Her eyes shone with the hope Sobers had seen, but her face remained calm. A steady, strong girl. "I want to know, one way or the other. If he's alive, no matter what he's done, I want to find him. Don't you want to know —for sure—what did happen to your wife?"

No doubts, no matter how small? No unanswered questions? Aware that if he came up with nothing this time, if it turned into an empty wild-goose chase, they could throw the book at him? A bail-jumper. A fugitive.

PART TWO

Down a Dark Road

10

They landed in San Francisco in a thin January rain. By the time they had rented a car and started north for Marin, the rain had become a steady downpour on the dark road.

"Butler told you he'd found your father?" Sobers said.

"No, he hadn't found him, but he was convinced he was still alive. Roy thought he was hiding, maybe had another name. So we came up here to look for him."

"Forbes prosecuted Glavin in 1959," Sobers said, watched the road in the rain, "but didn't marry your mother until 1963. They waited until Glavin's father died, left what he had."

"Yes," Gloria said. "But they didn't wait to get together. After my father went to prison, Henry moved down to San Vicente, went to work for Calixco."

"You didn't tell this to the sheriff?"

"I couldn't," she said. "Not until I know."

She couldn't betray her lost father, not yet. Sobers was sure the sheriff knew anyway, but with John Glavin dead, what difference did it make? Only if Glavin wasn't dead . . . ?

"Did anyone else know you were going up to Marin?"

"Not unless Henry or Roy told them."

"Then what makes you doubt it was Forbes who shot you?"

"If he did, it wasn't because of Roy and me. He knew I'd never marry Roy Butler."

A conflict was clear on her pale face in the dark car. Somewhere her real father might be alive, but she had lived all her life with Henry Forbes as her father. If Glavin were alive, why had he never come to her? Had Henry Forbes been the only 'father' who really loved her? Or had Forbes and Doris kept Glavin away from her? Forbes couldn't be a murderer, yet how could she think that her lost real father was? But if Forbes hadn't shot her and himself, who was shooting and killing?

"Why did Roy Butler dig it all up, Gloria? What did he expect to gain by telling you about it?"

"He wants to marry me. I suppose he thought he had to break me away from Mother to do it."

"Marry you? Because he's in love with you?"

Her laugh was clear and open. She was young, and even now she had to laugh when something was funny. Then she stopped.

"I don't know. I thought it was crazy at first, too, when he talked about marriage. Roy Butler! But then he worked so hard, tried to help, so I guess he meant it."

"But you don't want him? You just want your father?"

"I just want to know," she said.

Her voice was low, sincere. Sobers hoped it was the truth. He was a fugitive now, a bail-jumper, and if they wanted to get him they could.

*

It was after 8:00 P.M. in San Rafael, and the prosecutor's office was closed. The sheriff's office was open. San Vicente wouldn't have missed him yet. He hoped they hadn't, anyway. Lieutenant Kincaid was on duty. He was still friendly.

"Mr. Blake was prosecutor then. Retired six years ago."

"Can we talk to him?" Sobers asked.

While Kincaid got in touch with the retired prosecutor, Sobers and Gloria waited in the outer office. Deputies came in and out. Sobers watched them. Any instant they could get a call from San Vicente, swarm all over him. It was a feeling Sobers had never known. He was learning a lot he'd never known.

"Did you know my wife, Gloria?"

"I saw her once," she said. "With Roy."

"But he was in love with you? Wanted to marry you."

"I dropped him for a time. He had to have women."

"You weren't going to marry him, anyway."

"No," she said.

It was over an hour before Lieutenant Kincaid returned.

"Mr. Blake says he'll see you. He lives up near Novato. I'll mark a map for you."

*

In the cold rain they found the small house just off the dark road west of Novato. Mr. Blake was an erect old man with gray eyes behind steel-rimmed glasses. He nodded them to chairs near an open fire, sat filling a pipe.

"Henry Forbes was shot in San Vicente," Sobers said. "Can you tell us about the John Glavin case?"

Blake went on filling his pipe. "Glavin killed Walter Unger, a local businessman. Unger was with Glavin's wife, there was a fight in Unger's house, Unger died of a fractured skull. The wife called the police—Glavin's wife, that is, Unger was unmarried. Glavin was arrested at the scene, admitted both the fight and the motive. We charged second-degree murder, settled for a plea of

87

guilty to manslaughter."

"Who's idea was the reduced plea?"

Blake gave Sobers a withering glance. "Mine, of course. Henry Forbes had only two witnesses: Doris Glavin and Walter Unger's more regular woman, Sandra Innes. Doris Glavin was a hostile witness. Sandra Innes wasn't at Unger's house that night, could testify only that Unger had been seeing Mrs. Glavin and that Glavin had been looking for his wife. Glavin had been drunk, his confession was hazy and confused. Under the circumstances, the bargain was quite logical."

"Mr. Blake?" Gloria said. "Could my father be alive?"

The old man lit his pipe. "I don't see how. The Wyoming authorities knew of his parole, sent his fingerprints to us."

"Mistakes can be made," Sobers said.

Gloria sat staring into the crackling fire.

"What kind of man was Glavin, Mr. Blake?" Sobers said. "Could he kill?"

"He did kill."

"In a fight."

"I'm not a psychiatrist," the old man snapped.

"How did Glavin act back then?"

"Remorseful, ready to accept his punishment. Almost indifferent, as I recall. The wife fought for the reduced charge."

"You know that she and Forbes got married?"

"Yes." Blake's eyes flashed in the firelight. "I knew nothing about their affair until later, although it must have begun soon after Glavin's arrest. I would have fired Forbes at once. That he resigned was to his credit, if I didn't care much for where he went to work later."

"You mean Calixco Petroleum?"

"Forbes had prosecuted Calixco more than once."

"He switched sides? Isn't that almost standard now?"

88

"Not to me! I examined his cases very closely after he joined Calixco. I found nothing irregular, but I believe that a public official should be above suspicion. Henry Forbes failed on two counts. He was the best young man I ever had in my office, I expected much from him. I know better now. The best men go where the money and power are."

"Or where the woman goes?"

"Yes. Some women seem to specialize in sensitive men. John Glavin was a poet. Forbes was sensitive, too. He never really liked criminal prosecutions, hated to hurt people." Blake closed his eyes as if remembering Henry Forbes as he had been, and perhaps feeling suddenly mortal. "You suspect that John Glavin might be alive? That he could have murdered Henry Forbes?"

"It's possible," Sobers said.

"But that would not account for someone being interested in the Unger case some months ago, would it?"

"A man named Roy Butler?"

"Yes. He came to me in early November. A magazine writer, he said, who seemed to know Henry Forbes."

Gloria looked up. "What did you tell him, Mr. Blake?"

"What I've told you, and suggested that he contact a man named Josh Brady on North Beach in San Francisco. Brady was a character witness at the trial in 1959, knew the Glavins well."

"You have an address for Brady in North Beach?"

"No, but I do for Sandra Innes, Unger's lady-friend, if you want it. It's Twenty-four Sonoma Street in Nogales." Blake sighed in the warm room with the sound of rain against the windows. "A sad case, really. Unger was no great loss, and the Glavins were young. A mismatch, I think. The boy was too sensual, too dependent on a woman, and the rustic life didn't suit the wife. Glavin's father didn't help. He was an old man with rigid ideas—poetry was at best a hobby, not work for a man. They fought, and the wife sided with the father."

"He left everything to the wife when he died," Sobers said.

Blake nodded. "I suppose that could be motive for revenge."

*

Sonoma Street in Nogales was a dirt lane off one of the short side streets under the rain-shrouded mountains. Number 24 was a white cottage in a ragged, unfenced yard. It was dark, the garage was open and empty, and no one answered the door.

It was nearly ten o'clock, neither of them had eaten since lunch. The Redwood was the only motel in Nogales, but the old clerk would be sure to call Kincaid if he saw them, and Kincaid could have heard from San Vicente by now. Sobers drove back to the first motel on Highway 101. At the late hour the restaurant was empty. Sobers ordered a beer. Gloria had a martini, drank half of it in a long gulp.

"Are you hurting?" Sobers said.

"Not very much," she said.

They both ordered the daily special—chili with rice, and salad. Gloria drank her second martini more slowly.

"When Roy told me about it, about Henry sending my father to prison and marrying mother, it seemed so rotten, so dirty, such a cheat." She looked up at Sobers, her chopped-short hair and thin face making her look like an adolescent boy. "But I wasn't there, was I? I don't know how it really was back then, what happened to them all. Roy made it sound nasty, but when Mr. Blake talked it only sounded sad. A lot of mistakes, but no one really to blame."

She was very different from her mother. Serious, sen-

90

sitive, and almost unaware of herself. Perhaps she took after John Glavin—or Henry Forbes. What was more important, heredity or environment? She wasn't as beautiful as Doris Forbes, not even really pretty. The body of a woman, more curved now that she was thinner, but unaware of that, too. A big girl, awkward. Not at all like Susan.

"If only they'd told me!" she said. "If they hadn't lied to me all those years!"

"Would you have understood? You didn't a month ago."

"I suppose not." She drank. "Mr. Blake didn't like Henry taking the job with Calixco. Conflict of interest, right?"

"Among other things."

"Could that have been why he was shot, Paul? His business? I mean, maybe it wasn't anything about my father?"

"His boss, Otto Genseric, says no way. But . . . ?" Sobers shrugged, drank his beer. "There's no real way for a man in any government position today *not* to come up against conflict of interest. The businessmen seek him out, go after him, are always looking for an edge. The man in government is usually a businessman himself, one of them. He thinks like a businessman, and it's easy to think that what's good for business is best for the country. People who think different, like artists, scientists, professionals, don't go into government."

"What are you?" Gloria asked.

"Me?" He thought about what he was. "Sort of half-assed. An industrial designer. That's a professional semi-artist who works for businessmen. A kind of twilight zone that tends to sneer at the hands that feed us. Susan used to get angry about that. She said I was a businessman like everyone else. I had to work for businessmen, I should live like a businessman, and we should get our share."

"Were you very much in love with her, Paul?"

"I suppose I was. I don't think I realized it though, until she . . ." He finished his beer. "Sometimes people think they want different things than they have, but maybe in the end we all get what we really want whether we know it or not. I guess I didn't know how much I loved Susan until she left me, and . . ."

The waiter came with their chili then, and Sobers let it trail off. For a time they ate in silence. The chili wasn't very good, but they were hungry. Gloria finished first.

"We really want what we get whether we know it or not?" she said, poked at her salad. "Maybe my father wanted to fail, suffer."

"It can happen that way. Especially to artists, poets."

"Not to my mother. She knows what she wants. Gets it."

"Maybe she's the lucky one," Sobers said.

After their dinner they drove back to 24 Sonoma Street. The garage was still empty, but there was light inside. A woman in a gray cardigan answered their ring. She eyed Sobers.

"Miss Innes?" he said. "You knew Walter Unger eighteen—"

"They always want Sandra," the woman said.

"You're not Sandra Innes?"

"Maxine Innes. The men always did want Sandra. All except Walter Unger, eh? He wanted that classy blonde." She laughed, gleeful that her sister had lost Walter Unger eighteen years ago.

"Where is Sandra? It's important."

"How should I know?" She started to close the door.

"She could be involved in a murder," Sobers said.

Maxine Innes stared at him. "Murder? What murder?"

"Henry Forbes. The man who prosecuted John Glavin."

"That was eighteen years ago! Glavin's dead."

"Maybe he isn't, and someone killed Henry Forbes."

Maxine Innes was pale. "Sandra . . . she got a phone call about nine. She got dressed up, took the car."

"Did she say who it was had called?"

"No." Maxine Innes's eyes were suddenly afraid. "She . . . she said she'd be back in an hour."

Sobers looked at Gloria in the rain night. Nine o'clock was nearly three hours ago. Was someone ahead of them on the dark road? A killer?

11

Sobers woke up to bright sun and called Maxine Innes. Sandra still hadn't come home. The sister was almost hysterical when Sobers hung up.

He sat in the motel room and thought. By now the Marin police could easily have heard from San Vicente that he was a fugitive, a bail jumper. Ruston had certainly missed Gloria. But he had to take the chance. He called Lieutenant Kincaid. If Kincaid knew, they'd have to run.

"Sobers? How'd it go with Mr. Blake? Any help?"

"Can't say for sure," Sobers said into the receiver. It didn't sound as if Kincaid knew anything. He told him about Sandra Innes. "You better look for her. Call it a feeling."

"Where will you be?" Kincaid asked.

"I'll call you."

He hung up, dressed, and went out to knock on Gloria's door. The girl was ahead of him, already standing out in the clear, crisp mountain morning. She looked at the high sky.

"I could live here," she said.

"So could I," Sobers said. "I don't think Susan could have, though, any more than your mother."

"I guess people should be careful who they marry."

"Few ever are," Sobers said. "Sandra Innes still hasn't come home. We better get down to San Francisco, talk to that Josh Brady in North Beach."

*

North Beach was a neighborhood between two hills on the Barbary Coast of Gold Rush days. In the fifties it had been a home of the Beat—that first postwar youth rebellion with more dreams and less drugs than later, more revolution and less alienation. A rebellion that exposed, if not a flaw in the country, at least a conflict that led directly to peace marches, black power, hippies, Birchers, and, inevitably, backlash.

The narrow streets were the same, but the names and faces had changed. The Co-Existence Bagel Shop was a dress shop. Where the Bread and Wine Mission had been, there was a laundromat. The poetry readings, where listeners snapped their fingers instead of clapping, so that landlords couldn't evict the poets for noise, had moved on. Vesuvio's was still there, and Enrico's, but the crowds were different—tourists, Hell's Angels, derelicts, old Italians, and the Chinese from next door.

The Beat, like John Glavin, were gone—and yet not quite. The Trieste Café was there, and the survivors were still in it. Older now, and what they had found in the end seemed to be only a way of life and work they could live with. Still, that was more than many people ever found, and the circle of die-hards remained a community. When Sobers asked if they knew where he could find Josh Brady, they did.

It was the top floor of a shabby old building, and Brady was at work. A short, balding man in paint-stained overalls and a sweatshirt, Brady was painting an enormous canvas, and now Sobers recognized the name—J. Brady. Not a famous artist, but not unknown anymore, either.

"Johnny Glavin?" Brady said.

He put down his brush, poured a glass of wine from a gallon bottle, and offered them some. Sobers shook his head. Gloria took a glass. Brady stared at her as he pushed litter off a couch and some chairs. The room was large and old and full of the debris of a man who had lived long in the same place.

"More magazine writers?" Brady said. "I guess we still interest the straights. What wild things are those dirty Beats doing? Did we find something they might have wanted if they'd had the guts to try? Where are they now, those ancient rebels—dead, crazy, in jail, or just plain skid row drunks?"

"Where are they now, Mr. Brady?" Gloria asked.

"Where they always were," Brady said. "True to form *inside* like everyone else. The real artists are still artists somewhere. The one-in-ten real Bohemians are still Bohemians. The weak and sick are dead, the crazy are locked up, and the rest are back paying off the mortgage and waiting for the end. A little changed, the mortgage-payers, a little different."

"Which one is John Glavin?" Sobers asked.

Brady didn't answer, studied Gloria. "You're his kid. Johnny's girl, right? Gloria."

"Gloria," she said. "Yes."

"What makes you think Johnny's anything but dead?"

"A book of poems," Sobers said. "Some talk Gloria's heard, and maybe the murder of Henry Forbes."

"Forbes? When and how?"

"Shot three weeks ago in San Vicente," Sobers said. Brady drank his wine. "How's little Doris?"

"Scared, I think, Mr. Brady," Gloria said.

"Of Johnny?"

"Should she be?" Sobers said.

Brady went to pour more wine. "Twenty years ago it should have been the other way around. Johnny should have run screaming from Doris. A cute trick from a family of lace-curtain losers. Johnny was young, bright, and a poet. Doris's idea of a poet was Lord Byron and fame and fortune. She quit her job the day they got married and waited for the chariot ride to the top. Not odd jobs and poetry in damp cellars."

Brady drank. "Not that I blamed her for that, a lot of the women couldn't make the Beat scene, just faded away. Doris didn't fade, and that I blame her for—for hanging onto a man she didn't want."

"Perhaps she loved him," Gloria said.

"Maybe," Brady said, "but she resented his poetry. It was time away from *her.* She resented his odd jobs. An odd job was so he could write, a real job would have been for her. Nothing could be really important to him except her. No poet can give that and stay a poet. So she started looking for attention somewhere else, leaving Gloria with him. It tore him up, her playing around. He'd come and cry to me about it."

"Other men?" Sobers said. "Before they went to Marin?"

"That's why he took her up there, to isolate her." Brady looked out his high windows at his city. "Most people do nothing with their lives. Some swim with the current and end up on top. A few try to buck the current, change life, and end up who the hell knows where. Doris was a current-swimmer looking for the top. Johnny wanted to buck the current, but he didn't have what it takes. I guess Doris wasn't to blame. Johnny wasn't strong enough to beat her or weak enough to let her win, and she was too bright a woman to just accept what was."

"Is John Glavin alive, Brady?" Sobers asked.

Brady studied his wine. "About six months ago I got this book of poems from a small New York publisher. Johnny's poems. I remembered most of the early ones, but not the later ones. The style seemed the same, but the later ones were stronger, more mature, controlled. None of them were dated, but I just knew a lot of them had to have been written after 1966. There's a feel, an atmosphere of the seventies. Something about the attitude to events. I told this writer guy—"

"Roy Butler?" Gloria said.

Brady nodded. "He showed up in November, asked about the Unger mess. I gave him the book, said I had a hunch Johnny might still be alive. He went off to New York, but the publisher turned out to be an arty operator who'd never even met Johnny. He'd read some poems in a literary magazine, contacted the mag, and got the manuscript from a P.O. box. He didn't even know if Johnny was still alive, neither did the lit mag people. So Butler came back, went up to Marin again, and came down pretty excited. He pumped me all one night for anywhere Johnny might hide."

"Glavin could be hiding?" Sobers said. "Why?"

"Maybe because of his prison record. Maybe he's straight now, doesn't want anyone to know he's a poet. He could have a new name, a new life. He could be crazy. Or maybe he wants to cover his tracks. He took it hard back then, like he didn't really know what had happened. Maybe he—"

Brady stopped, emptied his wine glass in one motion.

"Maybe he what, Mr. Brady?" Gloria said.

"Josh," Brady said. "Maybe Johnny really *didn't* know what happened back then." He studied his empty wine glass. "At the trial they proved that both Unger and Doris came down here to San Francisco a lot. But, you know, no one ever really proved they came down here together. Unger was a small town slob, over forty, and a skirt chaser. He just wasn't Doris's type. A fling maybe, but an affair?"

"You think there was some other man?" Sobers said.

"What difference would it make?" Gloria said. "My father did find my mother with Unger, and he did kill Unger."

"He found Unger with her," Brady said, "and he killed him."

Sobers said, "When did you see Glavin last?"

"In 1965, right after he was paroled. Like a zombie, not writing and getting fat. He wanted money to go to Wyoming with some prison buddies and try to start writing again. One of the new pals came from Wyoming. I gave him money, that was it."

"Prison friends?" Sobers said. "Was one named Kapek?"

Brady thought. "It's a long time. The one from Wyoming, he was . . . Lacy, or . . . Tracy! Yeh, that was it. Jack Tracy from Green River."

*

Sobers sat on the jet to Cheyenne like a man who has heard the clang of a steel ring closing and has seen the dark depths of an abyss opening. Jack Tracy. A casual friend in need to a man whose wife had been murdered.

"Who is this Jack Tracy?" Gloria had asked.

He had told her, and on the plane now she sat and stared out the window at the Sierra Nevadas below.

"You think my father could have sent Tracy to San Vicente to do something?

"I don't know why Tracy was in San Vicente, except that it wasn't to sell pencils, and I don't think he was alone. That Frank Kapek was in Soledad with your father, too."

They landed in Cheyenne, rented another car, and Sobers called Lieutenant Kincaid in San Rafael. He was taking a chance by now, dialed direct. Kincaid took some time coming to the phone.

"Where are you, Sobers? The girl with you?"

Too quiet, too casual. San Vicente had called Kincaid.

"Have you found Sandra Innes?" Sobers said.

"No," Kincaid said and, "Sheriff Hoag called, Sobers. He's got a fugitive warrant out on you, a missing persons on Gloria Forbes. He's talking kidnapping, too. You better get back—"

"We've got something to finish."

There was a silence. "You and the girl don't like the answers they've got down in San Vicente?"

"Let's say we want to be sure."

"Is it worth what you're getting into, Sobers?"

"My wife was murdered!"

Kincaid was silent again. "Maybe you know what you're doing. We didn't find Sandra Innes, but we did find her car. It was abandoned on a back road two miles from Nogales. It was empty."

12

Sobers drove west out of Cheyenne across the winter plains. Snow stretched white as far as the eye could see. Deep snow that covered the eroded gulleys and lonely wire fences of the high, flat, almost deserted land. At eight thousand feet, it was higher than eastern mountains. A vast land without features, where a man could still vanish without a trace.

"Roy Butler gave you the book of poems, not Kapek?"

"Yes," Gloria said.

The highway and the railroad seemed to reach ahead into nowhere, and a few distant houses were lost in the emptiness.

"So Kapek didn't want the book found," Sobers said. "Why? Because your father is hiding, wants to stay 'dead'? Or is he really dead, and someone doesn't want anyone asking questions?"

"Roy was asking questions, wasn't he?"

"Yes," Sobers said.

"This Jack Tracy knew your wife?"

"So he said."

"And she knew Roy, was around him."

"Yes," Sobers said.

Dwarfed by the land, they drove on with the heater up full against the wind that swept snow in sheets across the highway. They passed through sudden gray towns little changed from the days men rode in on horses, walked on wooden sidewalks, and carried the Colts that made all men equal. The horses were pickup trucks now, the sidewalks were concrete, and the Colts were left at home, but the weathered buildings and people still huddled in the snow against the wind from the plains that forever threatened to blow them away.

"I feel so small out here," Gloria said. "So feeble." Her eyes seemed to follow the railroad tracks that went on and on beside the highway like an illusion. "That Mr. Brady said most of us do nothing with our lives. Is he right, Paul?"

"I guess that's up to each of us."

"He was right about my mother," she said. "She hasn't changed, always looking for the current to carry her on. Whatever's happening, she has to be part of it. Whatever everyone wants, she has to have. Not like Henry. He never seemed to want much of anything." She watched some far off black dots that were isolated cattle struggling to survive the winter. "Do you like Doris, Paul?"

"She's a dynamic woman."

"Like whirling lights," Gloria said. "That's how I used to see her when I was small. All glittering and moving. Eating up the air, changing, ready to fly away. Was your wife like that, Paul?"

"I'm not sure I ever knew what Susan was like." He drove. "Maybe that's what I'm really doing—trying to find out what Susan was like, what she wanted, what I didn't give her."

They passed few other cars, no one walked the high country in winter, and they reached Green River and the

Highway Patrol office. The town was no more than a few streets that climbed up from the railroad and the shallow river to eroded hills that would be a dusty ochre in summer, but that now belonged to the snow. The hills, streets, river, and town now belonged to the snow, and in the Highway Patrol office a sergeant and three civilians warmed themselves close to a glowing stove. Sobers told the sergeant what they wanted. The civilians looked at Gloria.

"Sure, back in Sixty-six, worst blizzard I ever saw," the sergeant said. "Pulled folks out of stalled cars everywhere. Ten died in the Uintas and over to the Wasatch. Don't recall—"

"Jack Tracy, sure," a civilian said. "Had a shack out on Blacks Fork, was livin' with some other guys. Lost six days out hunting 'fore they got found. Two died, I remember, and Tracy lost his legs."

"Was John Glavin or Frank Kapek one of those who died?"

The sergeant got up and began to dig through a filing cabinet. After a time, he came out with a thin folder.

"Here it is. Jack Tracy, he lost both legs. John Glavin and Frank Kapek were DOA, froze out there. The fourth guy, Ward, came through it okay."

"A fourth man?" Sobers said. "What was his first name? What happened to him? Where was he from?"

The sergeant shook his head. "Just says Ward, no address, no record of treatment or where he went. They was brought into the hospital here. Maybe they got some record."

"How were the dead men identified?" Gloria asked.

"Well," the sergeant read, "Tracy identified the dead guys, and they had parole papers from California. We sent their prints to Sacramento, got confirmation okay. Kapek had no next of kin, Glavin's ex-wife sent money

103

to bury him here."

"No one saw the dead men except Jack Tracy? No one who knew them? Just Tracy and their fingerprints?"

"All we needed," the sergeant said.

Sobers and Gloria left the four of them around the glowing stove, already talking about that great blizzard of '66. At the hospital the wind shook the windows as a woman in a wool skirt and boots looked up the old records.

"Jack Tracy," she read. "Both legs amputated above the knees, had trouble with artificial legs. Nothing at all on any Ward. You're sure this Ward came to the hospital?"

"Highway Patrol says he was brought in with Tracy."

The woman thought. "I remember that blizzard, hospital was swamped. If his case wasn't serious, I suppose Ward could have been treated without anyone getting his name. Maybe Tracy's sister would know more— Tracy was released to her back then. Mrs. Sarah Jared, Big Sandy Road, R.F.D. Twelve, in Granger."

*

A mile east of Granger, Big Sandy Road was a dirt track through a snow-covered gulley. Sobers drove aware of the hazards of snow, boulder, and ditch. The windows were half frosted even against the defroster, and they both became aware of their tiny heated space, the isolated beat of the car motor.

"We take our equipment for granted," Sobers said. "But out here a broken heater hose or flat tire could mean disaster."

"Or death. Is that how he died, my father? Some small accident, a trivial mistake?"

"Two men died, but which two? One was either Glavin or Kapek, but which one, and who was the second? A swamped hospital, confusion—and fingerprints can be substituted. What did Glavin look like, Gloria? Did he have any scars?"

"Doris showed me a picture of him just before he went to prison. He was a big man, tall and broad, but he had no scars."

Josh Brady had said Glavin had been getting fat in 1965, and a man could pick up scars in prison, physical and mental.

Sobers drove on expecting to see the shaggy bulk of a bear loom up out of the snow any second, but all he saw was the blowing powder of snow, as if the land itself were moving, until the lights of a house appeared directly ahead. A small house with an almost-buried mailbox: *Jared*. Sobers parked. A voice seemed far off on the wind. A woman's voice:

". . . out there?"

They stepped from the car, left the motor running. The cold almost took Sobers' breath away.

"Mrs. Jared? We came about Jack! Highway Patrol sent—"

The wind tore at his face, blew his shout.

". . . in! Hurry up!"

They stumbled to a raised doorway. A double doorway. Sobers fought the outer door closed, and the inner door opened. A bony woman stood framed in the light from inside. In her sixties, she wore a heavy sweater and held a rifle.

"What's your names?"

"Paul Sobers," he said, "and Gloria Forbes. We—"

She lowered the rifle. "Okay, Mabel called me from the hospital. Close the door."

They went into a neat living room of floral slip covers and rustic wood. Mrs. Jared poured mugs of steaming coffee.

"What's Jack done this time?"

Sobers took his coffee. "Why do you think that?"

"Good news waits 'til morning out here in January."

Gloria said, "We just want to ask about a friend of his."

"Bums and convicts!" Mrs. Jared snarled. "I tried to keep him here, give him a home, but he always was a fool. Going to be someone! Prison and no legs, that's what he is. Jared left me the house and a pension, and Jack could've had a job over to Westvaco doin' figures. Not him! He made them big shoes, and went off leavin' me flat."

"Eleven years ago?" Sobers said. "Where did he go? Have you seen him since?"

"Ten years ago," Mrs. Jared said. "He stayed here a year first, eatin' my food and bringin' in nothing. Then one o' his jailbird pals showed. Off they run to New York City, and I ain't seen nothin' of Jack since."

"John Glavin?" Gloria said. "Was his friend John Glavin?"

"Or Frank Kapek, or a man named Ward?" Sobers asked.

"Big man with a beard. Never heard no name, only saw him the one time—when he come to get Jack. Just walked off without leavin' me a dime. What's he do in New York, a useless cripple like him?"

"He's still in New York?" Sobers said. "You know where?"

"Sure. Number Twenty-three Grove Street, wherever that is. He writes me a letter once a year, but does he ever send any money? Just big talk!"

"What kind of big talk?" Sobers asked.

"All about some writer pal who's gonna be important, and Jack's gonna be important right with him. Rich and famous. Sure he is!"

They left the woman brooding in her spotless living room and went out through the snow to their car. When they reached the highway, Sobers turned east and drove fast toward Cheyenne. There was just time to make the last flight out for Chicago, and a connection to New York.

*

There was snow in New York, but it wasn't the same. In New York, for better or worse, man dominated, and even in the small hours there was traffic on the parkways as they took a taxi to Sobers' apartment on East Tenth Street.

They got out at the corner, approached his building warily, but no one was watching it. Sobers had hoped that Sheriff Hoag would have no reason to think he would go to New York, and the New York police had more to do than stake-out around the clock for a minor fugitive. They went up.

It was a small but elegant apartment.

"Our compromise," Sobers said. "I like the quirks of the Village; Susan liked the elegance of being near Fifth Avenue."

"Is that a compromise that ever works?" Gloria said.

He gave her one of Susan's nightgowns. It was too small for her. He saw the bandage on her shoulder and the long, tight curves of her young body. The swell of her belly under the thin cloth, and her full thighs. She gave him a small smile before she went into the bedroom.

"Paul? Thanks for helping."

She was thinking of her lost poet father. Of tomorrow. On the couch Sobers thought of yesterday—and of her. Maybe it was only coming home for the first time to an apartment that would never have Susan in it again.

13

Perhaps it was the noise of the city, or the cold after weeks in California, but Sobers was awake before 8:00 A.M.

He lay under the blankets on the couch and listened to the ceaseless rumble of the city. He looked slowly around the familiar room, and all at once it was a strange room. Her room, not his. Susan's room, and there was only emptiness in it. Had it ever been his room, too? He missed her, and that was the emptiness, but suddenly her room was an alien room, not really part of him.

He missed her—but had he loved her? He had lived here with her, but had she loved him? She had left him, and *had* he loved her? Was that what he wanted to find out after all? If he knew what had really happened to her, why she had left him and why she had died, would he know then if he had really loved her? When he knew what she had wanted, what she had gone to?

Or was he trying to find out what he wanted?

He looked toward the bedroom where Gloria slept behind the closed door, and he thought of Doris Forbes. A widow and a woman, not a girl. A woman like Susan.

Maybe a lot like Susan. The girl, Gloria, nothing at all like Susan.

He went on looking at the closed door of the bedroom, and became aware of the silence behind that closed door.

She had heard Jack Tracy's Grove Street address too.

He jumped up, crossed to the bedroom door, and peered in.

She was still there, curled under the blankets, soft and solid. He watched her regular breathing for a moment, then closed the door. He stood for a time in thought. Sooner or later, the police would come looking for him.

He dressed, and wrote a quick note: *Gone to check at my office, stay here until I return. Repeat—stay here. Paul. P.S. If the police come, you don't know where I am.*

He closed the outside door softly as he left.

*

His office was in the Union Carbide building on Park Avenue. He didn't go there. He went into a bar on Lexington Avenue and called his office.

"Mr. Maroldo, please."

Joseph P. Maroldo, vice-president and his boss.

"Hello?"

"Joe? Paul Sobers."

"Goddamn it! Where are you?"

"In New York. Why?"

"What the hell's going on, Paul? The cops were here; they want me to report right away if you show up!"

"Are they watching?"

"No, I don't think so. There was only one detective, he didn't seem very worried, but—"

"I'm in the Gold Rail on Lexington. I'll wait ten minutes."

Sobers hung up, found a spot behind a coat rack near the side entrance, and waited. Maroldo showed up in five minutes, sat down at a corner table. Sobers watched, but no one seemed to be following Maroldo. He went to the table.

"I didn't kill anyone, Joe," he said.

"What the hell did you do?"

Sobers told him. "So I'm a bail-jumper, a fugitive."

"Hell, they're just leaning on you, but you better go on back and play ball. A good lawyer, a little contrition—"

"It's not over yet, Joe. I have to know, be sure."

Maroldo was trim and tailored, out of place in the seedy bar. "They could play rough, Paul. Are you sure—"

"I'm not sure of anything, except that I'm not sure."

Maroldo nodded, uneasy. "You know how we all feel at the office, Paul. Susan was the same as one of us."

"I know how you feel, Joe."

"Whatever you want, need, just ask. Okay?" Maroldo had light brown eyes as neat and tailored as he was. "We have to go on. Work helps, Paul."

"Not yet."

"Mack is carrying too much with you away. He can't do your caliber of work anyway."

"Not yet, Joe."

"Sure," Maroldo said, sympathetic. "Paul, I'm going to tell you what I've never told anyone who worked for me before—you're good. You're unique, Paul. You have a skill at industrial design greater than most, and a sense of industrial design better than any. We need you, and we want you. All the way. I told Susan just that, once. She asked—"

"Susan? She talked to you about me? My work?"

"Over two years ago. She was concerned about the future, about what you wanted, and I told her—"

"Two years?" Sobers said. "She never mentioned that."

"Paul, I told her just what I've told you now. That you have it to go all the way. My job, and better. The top."

110

"Do I hear an *if* in there somewhere, Joe?" Sobers said.

"If you make the commitment, Paul. Play the game."

Sobers said nothing.

"We need you, Paul. We want you all the way. Only you've got to decide your priorities."

Sobers stood up. "Not yet, Joe."

*

Black clouds had come up to cover the winter sun, and new snow began to swirl over the older mounds when Sobers got out of the taxi on Grove Street.

Number 23 was one of the thousands of four-story brownstones in Manhattan that had once been the townhouses of single families. Most had been renovated into expensive apartments, or partitioned into cheap apartments and rooming houses. This one hadn't been. Rundown, it was still a single house with massive stone steps up to the parlor floor. It wasn't where Sobers had expected to find Jack Tracy.

From a doorway across the street, he watched the building. Shades were down on all the windows, and as the day turned as dark as night with the falling snow, six people went into the building. Men and women, all ages and colors, and all shabbily dressed. Over the next two hours, no one came out.

Sobers walked up to an apartment building at the corner of Bedford Street, then through the alley behind it. He climbed a fence into the backyards of the brownstones. The yard of Number 23 was littered with junk, a mound of torn mattresses piled up against the building wall. The ground floor windows were barred, but there were no shades at the rear. Sobers slipped up and peered inside. He saw only a deserted kitchen, heard the low hum of voices toward the front—and heard the steps behind him.

"You, man!"

There were three of them. One white and two black in the dark of the thickening snow. Boys. But slum boys who moved smoothly into position where there was no way for Sobers to escape. Silent and watching him.

"I'm looking for Jack Tracy," Sobers said. "To talk."

They moved on some signal he never saw.

He hit one of them, knocked him back. One hit him in the stomach. One hit him in the face. The third came back . . .

Sobers was down in the new snow. An iron pipe lay on the ground. He grabbed for it. A foot stomped on his wrist. Two knives gleamed in sudden light from a doorway.

"Cap! Sancho!"

A woman was framed in the light of the open rear door of Number 23. She wore heavy slacks and a wool shirt over a denim shirt. Her face was hidden in shadow, but a solid woman, commanding. The three boys looked at her the way a cat crouched over a mouse looks at its owner—alert, wary, defiant.

"He was peepin', Doc! In your windows."

"Sneakin' around."

"Lookin' for Jack."

The woman stepped out into the falling snow, took the two knives out of their hands, and threw them away. The three boys turned and vanished as suddenly as they had come.

"Are you hurt?" the woman said. She looked after the boys.

"No," Sobers said.

"You better come inside."

They went into the kitchen and through three sparsely furnished rooms where people were reading or writing or grouped in hot discussion. No one paid any attention to Sobers as the woman took him into a small

112

side room and shut the door.

"So. You're looking for Jack Tracy?"

"Just to talk to him. We met—"

"You couldn't come to the front door?"

"I wasn't sure what this place was."

"What did you think? A brothel? A bomb factory?"

Her commanding manner wasn't arrogant, simply blunt and direct. She wore no make-up, and her graying hair was tied back by a rubber band. In her late forties, she had a round, almost motherly face. There was nothing motherly about her sharp eyes.

"Those boys out there called you 'Doc'," Sobers said.

"Titles are important to street kids. It's only a Ph.D., mostly in ignorance." She sat down, waved him to a seat, and seemed suddenly weary. "I'm sorry, Mr.—"

"Paul Sobers," he said, sat on a ragged couch.

"Elizabeth Price," she said and sighed. "It's slow, delicate work trying to tame those boys, bring out the talent they have in them despite the deprivation and violence they've lived with all their lives. Call us a kind of club, Mr. Sobers, and a haven. A literary club for the inarticulate, voices for the unheard. We teach, talk, listen, try to help them give their answers—and questions—through art. What life has shown them."

"Literary club? You mean poetry, stories? Where does Jack Tracy fit into that? Is he a poet, maybe?"

"You've come from California, Mr. Sobers?"

"What makes you think that?"

"Jack was out in California recently."

"Any special reason he went there, Mrs. Price?"

"I have no idea, and Jack isn't here. Perhaps you—"

"Actually," Sobers said, "I'm really looking for a man named John Glavin. A friend of Tracy's, and a poet."

He watched her for a reaction.

"The name is vaguely familiar."

It was all the reaction he got.

"Does your club publish a magazine, maybe? Literary?"

"Yes, we do. A small thing, I doubt that you know it."

"Maybe it published some of Glavin's poems."

"As a matter of fact, I think it did. Over a year ago, but our editor isn't here, either, so I think you had better come back. This is an entirely volunteer effort, we all have other employment, so it is difficult to be sure when any one of us will be here. Perhaps later this evening or tomorrow."

It was more than a helpful suggestion or two, it was a dismissal. Mrs. Elizabeth Price wasn't going to say any more. Sobers went out the front way this time. On Grove Street the snow fell thickly. He walked to the corner and around it in case he was being watched from Number 23. Once out of sight, he circled the block and returned to the alley on Bedford Street.

He slipped along the alley again, watching the shadows this time in the soft silence of the city snow, and crouched low as he approached the back of Number 23. Through the barred rear window the kitchen was still empty, and the back door had not been relocked.

Inside, Sobers listened to the voices from the front. To the left, beyond a bare pantry, stairs led upward. Narrow, servants' stairs from when the old house had been the home of some affluent Victorian. Sobers went up to the parlor floor.

On the carpeted parlor floor landing there was no sound at all. Nothing but voices below, and . . . somewhere above. Voices talking higher up, faint and far off. Isolated voices.

Sobers climbed softly to the third floor. Here the hallway was narrow, with doors opening off both sides. The voices seemed to come from a middle room. He listened

114

but couldn't make out any words. He knocked. There was no response. He opened the door and stepped inside.

It was a sitting room, with couches and chairs in the dim light of a single lamp. Jack Tracy sat in one of the chairs, his elephant-like stumps high off the floor.

"You did some lying out in San Vicente," Sobers said.

"A little, yeh," Tracy said.

"I want to know! About Susan. About—"

"Susan I don't know no more than you."

The hand gripped his neck and throat from behind. Silent and powerful. Hands that bent him backwards, lifted him, tall as he was, squeezed . . .

"Sorry, you know?" Jack Tracy said.

Roaring noise . . . red and green lights . . . black . . .

14

Somewhere there was a groan.

Like a cannon in Sobers' ears! He tried to shrink away, to hide. If they heard, they would come back!

Again the groan, and there was nowhere to hide, and it was his own groan. Stop it! Hide! Chained to a wheel where the executioner would soon break all his bones as the crowd cheered his screams.

Where had all the voices gone? The soft footsteps that filled the dark?

He opened his eyes. His neck hurt, and his throat. His wrists hurt, and his ankles. He was tied. Not on a wheel. In a chair out in the center of a dark and empty room.

Only one man could have had those hands.

Somewhere now. Where? Near or far?

Hands that could snap his neck like a chicken.

Strapped in an execution chair.

Somewhere the sounds of the city, the hiss of wheels distant and far apart. Late night in the city.

Strapped rigid, he waited.

*

Far off a laugh, high and female.

Closer, the clink of a glass. The scrape of a chair. A match that scratched alight. In another room.

Voices in another room. Low and insistent. Words without shape or meaning that circled through the clink of glasses. Voices that went on and on and on.

*

The hissing rumble of a bus that rocked light and empty in the snow.

So near, the city, and so far. Asleep body to body. Unaware of the monsters that loomed in the night in empty rooms. Unaware of a man in a chair so near and yet so far.

A man who could be dead in a chair in an empty room. Unknown.

A man whose neck could be snapped in faceless hands, his body flung into a corner as the unknown door closed on heavy feet that died away along a dark and silent corridor.

*

Air on his face. Something moved.

The undulation of terror softly moving like the air itself through the dark room.

Someone in the room.

A quick, erratic shadow in emptiness. Behind him. Breath on his neck. The rigid ache of his naked neck that waited for the edge. Sharp, hot breath close to his neck. Fingers.

Cold nicked his neck warm with blood. A knife!

His hands were free. His feet were free.

"Can you stand?" A female whisper.

"No."

"Try!"

He swayed on the cramps of his legs, and Elizabeth

Price held him. They stood shivering together.

"You have to!"

He stepped. Once. Twice. A metallic robot.

"I think I can now," he said.

"Go down the front stairs and out the front."

Air moved again, she was gone.

*

In the dark of the third floor hallway, Sobers listened to the singing. Low and soft back toward the rear. A slow, weary song. The lonely sound of a man singing to himself.

He looked down the carpeted stairs that faded away into the shadows below. Was he a hardhead? A stubborn idiot? Yes. He still had a murdered wife to do something about.

He walked to the rear of the silent corridor. Behind the closed door of the last room the singing stopped. His hand shook on the knob as he opened the door.

It was a spartan room with a cluttered desk, a wooden chair, steel shelving full of narrow, brightly colored books, a single lamp, and a double bed. A man lay diagonally across the bed, face down. The giant man in dirty Levis and a red wool shirt.

"Kapek?" Sobers said. "What are you scared of?"

"Wasting your time. No apologies."

His voice was thick, muffled.

"Apologies for what?"

"I get drunk. Beautiful. Go away."

"Are your poems better when you're drunk?"

Slowly the shaggy head turned. Sobers saw one red eye shining back toward him.

"You're not Elizabeth. Hell, no. Definitely not Elizabeth. Too tall." The eye closed. "Go away. Go now. Go fast."

For an instant, Kapek's thick voice became sharp and

118

clear. Sobers looked quickly around. But no one else was there.

"You live here? With Mrs. Price and Jack Tracy?"

The big man's face was down in the pillow again. "I hit you, right? For that you get the apology. Definitely."

"That was three weeks ago. In California."

"California? Think of that."

"You took the books of poems. Why?"

"Beautiful, poems. Say it clean, tell it true, bang your goddamned head upstream. Booze, that's all downstream. A nicer way to drown."

Sobers heard the twisted echo of Josh Brady out on North Beach. Was it one of those unconscious tracks left by the past in all of us, the small memories that give us away every time we speak our thoughts if the right person is there to hear? The big man's hoarse voice spoke in a mixture of rough grammar and big words. It could be the mark of a self-educated wanderer like Frank Kapek. Or it could be the reverse—an educated man who taught himself to hide his education to survive in prison.

"You didn't give that book to Gloria Forbes," Sobers said. "A man named Roy Butler did. Butler was tracing John Glavin, was tracking him down because he thought Glavin could be still alive. Someone tried to shoot Butler, shot Gloria Forbes instead. Someone shot Henry Forbes. Gloria Forbes is John Glavin's daughter. You didn't want Glavin's poems found in her apartment. Why?"

The big man rolled suddenly onto his back. That amazing speed of movement. Effortless, despite his size.

"John Glavin died," he said.

"There were three men," Sobers said. "A drifter named Ward, Frank Kapek, and John Glavin. Only two died."

The big man reached to a bed table for a cigarette. He

lit it. "You like that San Vicente place?"

"A nice town," Sobers said. "Two died in that blizzard. One was that drifter, Ward, I'm sure of that. Who was the other? Frank Kapek, or John Glavin?"

"Nice and neat, San Vicente." Ashes from the cigarette dropped into his beard unnoticed. "They know who they are, where they're going, and what they want. Sure, someone told 'em. No poets out there, no way. Poets look for what's true, not what someone told 'em was true. See and tell. Only in a place like San Vicente that's a big order. Those people long ago agreed to believe that what they was told made them nice, and safe, and comfortable."

"Ward and Kapek died, didn't they?" Sobers said. "You wanted people to think you were dead. Or was it only Doris and Henry Forbes you wanted to think you were dead? Maybe Gloria?"

The big man smoked on the bed in the light of the single lamp, letting the ashes fall anywhere, and suddenly shivered as if he could still feel the cold of that Wyoming blizzard. "They were dead, it was all over for them. Everyone was busy saving Jack. The hospital was jammed, the morgue chaos. No sweat to switch papers, switch fingerprints. Who knew Ward? That wasn't even his real name."

"So you buried John Glavin," Sobers said, "but Glavin went on writing, too. You buried Frank Kapek, but out in San Vicente you were Kapek. Buried both and became both. Why?"

The big man stared up at the shadowed ceiling. His shaggy head moved rhythmically back and forth, and his red-rimmed eyes looked at something beyond the room. "One man lived. What do the names matter? The past died, was buried, but the poet went on. The work went on—seeing it and telling it."

120

"You buried the past? A bad marriage and prison? Then why not kill the name, too? Write under a new name?"

"John Glavin is the poet!"

Sobers watched him. "Except in San Vicente. Except when the shooting started. Then Glavin had to be 'dead' again."

Sobers moved closer. "No, you had more in mind when you 'died' out there in Wyoming. Revenge. Some plan to get back what had been taken from you. Not legally, you couldn't do that. But when Gloria came of age, if her 'parents' died and her long lost real father suddenly appeared, maybe then—"

"Go away now, Sobers. You hear?"

"Did someone make a mistake? Print your new poems before you were ready? A publisher saw them, wanted to do a book, and who can resist a book of his work? Not a man who wanted to bury the past but couldn't bury his name! You probably convinced yourself that after all these years no one who knew anything about John Glavin would read an obscure volume of poetry. But Josh Brady read them, showed the book to Roy Butler, and when Butler started snooping too close it forced your hand. You had to act."

On the bed the big man closed his eyes. "You think I shot them?"

"You had the reason. Forbes sent you to prison and married Doris. They took what should have been yours."

"Wife and property. That too. The good wife and the honest lawyer." His eyes opened in the gloomy room, stared at some vision of horror in a dark corner. "Jesus God, what they did!"

"Forbes stole what was yours, and Doris—"

The big man sat up sharply. "Shut up! Sobers—"

Drag . . . clump . . . drag . . . clump . . . The sound was

121

a breath of ice in the room. Sobers tried for the door.

Grotesque on his elephant feet, Jack Tracy stood in the doorway, a pistol like a toy in his powerful hands.

"Get him," Tracy said.

The big man came off the bed, stumbled.

Sobers jumped back.

The gun fired.

A violent, searing blow to his head hurled Sobers back to the wall. A wall that wasn't a wall.

He felt the glass and thin wood against his back at the same instant he crashed through the high window and pitched out into the soft falling of the city snow.

He fell like a wingless eagle through the snow.

Aware that this was the end, the answer to all the questions. The end of Susan, of . . .

And hit soft in the center of the mound of old mattresses buried in new snow against the building wall. Hit, bounced, and slid down the slope of snow to lie sprawled on the thickening white blanket that covered the hard earth.

How long he lay there he never knew.

A sporadic car moved somewhere. A solitary bus hissed through the snow with the speed of emptiness. An isolated window showed light like the eye of a Cyclops. The rest of the great city dark and asleep, oblivious to terror that hovered in the early hours of morning.

Sobers became aware of himself walking through the alley behind the building on Bedford Street. His legs cold and wet through torn trousers. Blood in his eyes. Blood that dripped from the furrow high on his head. He pressed his hand to the bleeding, to the pounding of pain.

On Bedford Street no one walked.

A car cruised slowly in Seventh Avenue snow. Was gone.

At Sheridan Square the subway entrance yawned, invited, and Jack Tracy was there! Between Sobers and the subway.

Jack Tracy ten feet in the air like a giant in the night! Riding on a giant horse, his mouth open and shouting but without sound, the words blown away on the wind. A violent Cossack on a breath-streaming horse that was the big man. Tracy high on the shoulders of the massive, shaggy John Glavin.

Sobers lurched back into the darkness of Grove Street. A taxi stood near Number 23. Its door flung open:

"Paul! Here!"

He fell into the cab, buried his bleeding face in Gloria Forbes's full breasts. The taxi lunged away through the snow.

A cry of rage carried from behind on the wind.

15

The thing in the cold drawer was the demon of the dark waiting for him, Susan, his wife, who wanted to know his future. All the way to the top, Paul, if we all play the game. Strike three, *sayonara!* With dripping claws and the face of Roy Butler, the demon leaped into an explosion of light!

"How do you feel?" Gloria Forbes said.

A dazzling light seared at his eyes, slashed them, but he forced them open—anything to escape the dark where the demon waited. Even face a light too bright.

"Scared," Sobers said.

"It's not a bad wound," she said. "You're all right."

He was all right. Except that Susan had talked to his boss about his future, and John Glavin was alive. Except that he was a fugitive, and he had never seen this room he lay in before.

He sat up. "Where the hell are we?"

"The Hudson Hotel."

He lay down again, nauseous, his head pounding. He breathed slowly, controlling the nausea rising in his throat.

"Why?" he said.

"The police came to the apartment after you left."

She sat in a worn armchair beside the bed, her short coppery hair catching the bright sunlight reflected from the snow beyond the single window of the narrow room. Her eyes were tired, but her long, elegant face shone with the resilience of youth. She wore a Newmont College sweatshirt and Levi cords, and with the hospital-cropped hair looked like some surf-riding Huck Finn a long way from home. A female Huck Finn, the tight corduroys proving it.

"I slept late," she said, "and then waited a long time for you to come back. You didn't come, I got hungry and went out to get some food. That's when the police came. I heard them, saw the uniforms below, and hid up on the next floor until they went into your apartment. Then I slipped out. After I got something to eat, I watched the apartment from outside, waiting for you. It got awful late, you didn't come back, and I got mad."

"I'd expected to get back to you sooner," he said. He tried to smile, comfort her, but the nausea rose through him in waves, and he could think of nothing else for a time.

"You'd gone to Grove Street without me! I suddenly knew," she said, angry in memory. "So I took a taxi over there. But the whole building was dark, and I was afraid to look around alone. I sat in the taxi a long time just watching. Then I heard shots, and those two men came out—one riding on the back of the other! I knew something was wrong, was going to tell the taxi to circle the block when I saw you."

"Lucky for me," Sobers said. His head felt light, and his vision blurred as he smiled at Gloria. He touched his head. The hair had been shaved, and a neat bandage covered high up.

"I found a doctor," Gloria said. "He was a nice old man, said you'd be all right. A mild concussion. I gave him a false name, said we'd been mugged, and we slipped out while he was reporting to the police. We couldn't go to your apartment because of the police, and I didn't know if maybe those two men knew where you lived, too, so I came here."

"We're both learning," Sobers said. His head seemed to float, spin in the sunny room.

"Those two men, Paul. Was one Jack Tracy?"

"The ways of violence, the tricks," he said. "We're learning how to be suspicious and cunning. Two ordinary people, Gloria! What the hell is the world doing to us?"

He felt her hand soft on his brow as the room spun and darkened, her voice soothing and fading away . . .

*

The single window was dark. Sobers looked slowly around the small room. Gloria stood at the dark window looking out. He sat up. The remnants of a meal stood on a table.

"I guess I passed out," he said.

"All day." She turned from the window. "Was he there, Paul? At Grove Street? My father?"

He lay back against the headboard. He felt a lot better. But he didn't feel better for her. Sooner or later she had to know.

"I think so," he said. "Yes."

She crossed the room and sat in the armchair near the bed.

"What is he like?" She didn't look at Sobers.

"You already know," he said. "He's Frank Kapek, Gloria. The real Kapek is buried out there in Wyoming."

She sat silent in the armchair as the city lay muted outside in the snow. Hushed and slow, paralyzed under the power of nature.

"Frank Kapek?" she said, her eyes seeing the big, hairy man in her mind. "I wondered a few times why he was so friendly. He didn't seem to want anything from me. Just a stranger passing through, doing nothing and going nowhere."

"I suppose that's what he tried to seem like."

"Yes," she said, but she wasn't hearing Sobers. "He was nice, Paul, I liked him. He wasn't the kind of man I'd ever known before. Rough, dirty, but I liked him. He didn't seem like a father, not anyone's."

"Maybe he had things on his mind," Sobers said.

She stood up, went to the table where the dishes and food were. "You should eat something. There's a ham sandwich and milk. The sandwich is a little stale, and the milk's warm—"

"Bring it over. I'd eat the table now." He was suddenly starving. A sign of health, the demon of the dark gone.

She brought the sandwich and milk and sat down again.

"What happened at Grove Street?" she asked.

He told her as he ate. Her face was gray in the room.

"It was Tracy," she said. "Tracy tried to kill you."

"Tracy shot," he said, "but both of them grabbed me, tied me to that chair. Together, Gloria."

"But my . . . !" She held to the chair. "Glavin didn't try to hurt you. He didn't do anything except help Tracy. Perhaps he even tried to help you, warn you!"

"What do you want me to say, Gloria?"

She hunched in the chair. If there had been a fire in the room in the snowy night, she would have stared into it. But there was no fire in the drab and barren room of the cheap hotel, and she stared at something inside as she sat hunched, a shine at the corners of her eyes where tears waited.

127

"He's my father, but he's a stranger. I don't know him. I don't know what he's done. I don't know why he hid all these years, why he's still hiding. I don't know what he wants."

"Then we'll have to find out," Sobers said.

She brushed at her eyes, but if there had been tears, Sobers hadn't seen them. She remained hunched in the chair, a big girl in a college sweatshirt who looked now as if her college days had been long ago.

"What do any of us want?" she said. "What do you? What do I?"

"I want to know what happened to Susan, and you want to know who your father is. Or you want to know what happened to your father, and I want to know who Susan was."

"Or who we are?"

"Maybe that, too."

She took a deep breath, long and slow. "Why did she leave you, Paul? Your wife."

He finished the sandwich, drained the milk container, and looked for a cigarette. He couldn't find any on the bed table. Gloria went to the closet, brought back his crumpled pack, sat down again and watched him. He smoked.

"She said she had to find herself, become a person," he said. "I guess I'd thought she was a person, and I didn't know she was lost. But that was me, not her. I suppose I never knew the person she'd lost. I suppose she had to find something she didn't have. Maybe just Roy Butler."

"He's my father," Gloria said. "Why didn't he ever look for me?"

"Roy Butler or something. Something more than me. Or different, I suppose."

"You don't know why," Gloria said. "I don't know why."

128

"My boss is a vice-president of the company I work for, smart and smooth, plays the game. Susan talked to him about my future, where I was going as an industrial designer." He smoked for a time, watching the dark window of the bare room. "When I married Susan I had my own free-lance business. It was small, I operated out of my apartment. But I couldn't seem to make enough for us to live on, so I took the job with Future Forms. The money was a lot more, with a lot of fringe benefits and a lot of status. But what I wanted was the contacts so I could go back to my own business and do better. I planned to save money, quit Future Forms, and go run my own office again—maybe out in the desert. I talked about that to Susan all the time. She never said anything against it, so I thought she wanted it, too."

Hunched again in the chair, her eyes watched the floor. "Didn't she?"

"She never objected, but when I think about it now, she never talked about it either. I talked about working less, needing less, wanting fewer 'things,' a simpler life. She talked about promotions, more money, more 'things.' She liked the big money at Future Forms, the status, the things money and status brought. You can't have all that without playing the company's game, and I talked about quitting and the desert."

She raised her eyes, a gleam in them. "You think she left you because she wanted bigger things? Money and power and status? How? A lab technician in San Vicente? Roy Butler? What did he have to offer? Half the time I paid for our dates."

"A schemer, Tracy called him. Maybe he has plans, hopes. Something he talked about, told you?"

"All he talked about was us, me. Bed and marriage."

In the night outside the cheap room, trucks plowed the snow into piles and hauled it away. Clanking bulldozers and steel-toothed scoops freeing the city. Gloria got up and walked to the window, tall and restless in the loose sweatshirt and tight corduroys.

"Some people are always chasing more, aren't they?" she said. "The new. Running for more, another small triumph. It keeps them going, but they're never really content. Only change gives them a sense of winning, but change is also a loss, because it means that what they had chased earlier wasn't enough. So they go on chasing for more even when they don't need it."

"You're too young to know that," Sobers said.

"Am I?" She went on looking out the dark window. "I've seen it all my life. In my mother. Doris can't stop moving for more, she can't rest, enjoy what she has. She doesn't need more money or things, and most of the time she doesn't even like doing what she does, but she can't stop. When she sees something she can get, or money she can have, she can't stop working for it if she needs it or not." She watched something outside the high window for a moment. "I guess that's what really happened up in Marin back then. My father had found all he wanted, but Doris wanted more, had to change."

"Maybe," Sobers said. "Only then he lost it all, didn't he? Your father? He lost Doris, too. Maybe he wants it back."

She put her hand on the window glass as if she wanted to feel the cold. "It's not just Doris. Dr. Taylor is like that, believes it's what moves the world, the always wanting more. He's made Peter believe it. My . . . Henry, he was different. He used to say that wanting too much, getting too many 'things,' brought its own destruction, because once we have them we have to keep them. Soon everything we do is to keep what we have instead of using it, enjoying it."

"You don't think the same as Peter Cole?"

130

"I'm not sure anymore. Do you know that he's a photographer? A very good one, he could be an artist. But Dr. Taylor . . ." She raised her head, stared out the curtainless window. "Out there they work all their lives for apartments, furniture, 'things.' Day in and day out, but not an hour for passion, for touch and taste. Perhaps you can't care about both furniture and passion. Worst of all are all those out there who don't really care about furniture, but who never had the courage to reach for passion. Cardboard people waiting for nothing."

Sobers watched her back. "Playing the game. It's easier that way. The boat doesn't get rocked."

"Easier?" she said. "For who?" She turned to look toward him on the bed. "I told Peter once that maybe it's not what you do that matters, but how you do it. Do the job, but do it your way. If your work is needed, you don't have to play the game."

"Perhaps Peter is wrong for you," he said.

At the window, she didn't move for a time. Then she came to the bed. She sat down beside Sobers, bent and kissed him. He held her. She was both soft and hard, a young girl.

"I'm too old, Gloria," he said.

"That's up to me."

"No it isn't. The future is for both of us."

"Paul—?"

"Not now," he said. "Not here."

She closed her eyes, lay down on the bed beside him, her hand tight in his. Comfort in a cheap hotel room. Learning that, too, in a violent world.

The sound came from beyond the door.

. . . *drag . . . clump . . . drag . . . clump . . .*

16

Sobers pushed Gloria off the bed. On the far side, away from the door. He slid down beside her behind the bed. He watched the room door. Gloria watched him.

The sound neared the door outside . . . *drag* . . . *clump* . . . *drag* . . . *clump* . . . and passed on, a woman's voice singing low as she passed. Sobers stood up:

"A hotel maid. Dragging something."

"You thought it was Tracy," Gloria said.

Vertigo gripped Sobers, he had been lying in bed too long with the deep flesh wound in his head. He sat down on the bed, held to it.

"You're afraid of them, Tracy and my father," Gloria said. "You think they killed Henry and your wife, shot me."

"So do you," Sobers said. "You've been afraid of that all along."

"No! I was wrong. Not just for what happened. It's not enough, Paul! Not after eighteen years."

He lay back on the bed. "What if there was more, Gloria? Something else that happened back then. Something worse."

"Worse?" she said.

"When I told Glavin I thought he had reason to kill Forbes, maybe Doris, too, because they took his wife, his inheritance," Sobers said, "he said, 'Wife and property, that too.' Then he seemed to see some awful vision and said, 'Jesus God, what they did!' He looked like a man seeing some horror, some dark monster. Maybe something to make him hide and dream of revenge for all those years."

She left the bed, began to gather the used dishes and cartons from the table. Sobers watched her for a time, the noise of the city reviving again outside the room. Even snow can't control the great city for long. Sobers shivered, the room cold.

"Something a lot worse," he said. "What I can't quite understand is why he waited and why he moved now?"

"I'll make some tea," Gloria said. "I bought tea bags."

She filled a pan from the small sink, began to boil the water on the gas hot plate.

"What triggered him now?" Sobers said. "Roy Butler nosing around, digging up the past? Afraid Butler would find him, tell that he was still alive?"

She watched the water, readied two cups with tea bags.

"If they were murdered, the police would look at the past. The motive would be there, but not if Glavin was dead. But if he were alive, if Butler found out and told? No, he had to be dead for his revenge, Gloria."

The water boiled, she poured it into the two cups. She stirred the brew for a time and carried his cup to him. He was staring up at the ceiling, seeing what had happened.

"He had to stop Butler, and he tried—twice, it looks like." He sipped the hot tea, feeling warm again, sure. "But he missed, and then he had to act before Butler

133

warned anyone. He shot Forbes with Forbes's own gun. He must have stolen it earlier, part of the plan. Your house had once been his home; he knew it, could find the gun there without being seen. He had to have had the gun earlier to shoot Susan with it."

"You told me he couldn't have shot Henry," Gloria said. She held her tea. "You said the police told you Frank Kapek was in bars on the west side all that night."

"Someone must have lied," Sobers said. "A different gun shot you in Marin. That must have been Tracy, two together."

"Why would he shoot your wife?"

"Trying to kill Butler. Or there could have been some other reason. I know now that she wanted more than I gave her. More than I ever would give her."

Gloria sat holding her cup of tea, saying nothing now as it grew cold in the drab hotel room. Sobers finished his, felt the warmth inside, and thought about Susan. Different people, with different needs, and that was why she had gone from him. To find what she knew she could never find with him: her dreams not his dreams. Her . . . hopes . . . not . . . his . . .

*

The demon of the dark was shaggy now. A shaggy demon laughing at him, the hump of an elephant on its back. Riding out of the bright glare of the sun. A golden sun . . .

Sobers sat up.

Wide awake in an instant, he sat up in the bed, and the sun streamed in at the single window. An afternoon sun.

His teacup was on the bed table. The bed beside him was cold. The room was empty. Only the brisk sounds of the city outside, released from the grip of the snow.

"God damn!"

He jumped up. His head was steady, clear. He stared

134

at the teacup and saw the piece of paper under it. *"Yes, I drugged the tea. Sleeping pills they gave me in the clinic. I'm sorry. I have to face him myself, talk to him, ask him. I have to, Paul, I've waited so long. Understand. Please."*

Cursing, Sobers found his clothes. He understood, yes, but did she?

Dressed, he ran out of the barren room.

A daughter John Glavin hadn't seen or cared about for eighteen years! Did she understand the danger?

He waved for a taxi in the weave and jostle of the New York street. By the time a taxi stopped, he had stopped waving. He got in slowly, gave the Grove Street address.

Or was there any danger for her?

A daughter John Glavin *had* seen a lot more recently than eighteen years ago. Not much more than a month ago. Had she been surprised to learn that Frank Kapek was John Glavin and her long lost father? Or was he, Sobers, the one being led blind along a dark road?

*

The snow was piled in fresh mounds on Grove Street, and Number 23 looked empty behind its drawn shades. No one went in or out. Sobers knocked at the street-level door. After a time he heard footsteps, and Elizabeth Price opened the door.

"You lied," Sobers said. "Tracy was here all the time."

She looked at his head and looked away.

"He was scared," she said.

"So was I," Sobers said. "John Glavin was here, too. You were protecting them. Why?"

"I didn't know they would—!"

Sobers pushed inside. "I want to see them now!"

"They're not here. No one is here. You can look if you like."

She stepped back to let him walk through the silent rooms. Wearing the same slacks and wool shirt—a

135

woman who wasted no time on clothes—her face was tense. Sobers watched her.

"Where's the girl?" he asked.

"Girl?"

"Gloria Forbes, Mrs. Price. She came here this morning, I know that. Gloria Glavin once, his daughter."

"I told you there was no one here now."

"Did they take her with them?"

She looked away in the dim hall. "Yes."

"Where are they, Mrs. Price?"

She shook her head. "I can't tell you. You have no—"

"Yes I do! If they've taken Gloria, that's kidnapping!"

She walked down the hall and into a small room cluttered with books and manuscripts strewn on desks. Sobers followed her. She stood over a desk, touching the manuscripts as if they were alive.

"Not if she went willingly, Mr. Sobers," she said.

Had Gloria gone willingly?

"They've killed two people, Mrs. Price, maybe three," he said. "They could kill again if they're not stopped."

Elizabeth Price sat down. She folded her hands in her lap. Stained hands that did work. She sat very straight.

"You mean Johnny's first wife and her husband. Because he went to prison. That was a long time ago, Mr. Sobers. He's not the same man. He escaped all that when he pretended to die in the blizzard. He has a new life."

"A hidden life. Maybe cover for safe revenge."

"No, not Johnny."

"Then why did he go out to California?"

She searched her shirt for a cigarette. She didn't find any. Sobers gave her one of his, lit it.

"A few months ago Virgo Press called our magazine. Someone had been inquiring about Johnny. Some man from California."

"The publisher knew Glavin was here?"

"No, only that we'd published his poems and that Jack had sent the book manuscript to them. Johnny's name never appears on the magazine, and Jack makes any contacts. Johnny must have his time to work, his privacy."

"They went to California after the publisher contacted them about the man asking questions?"

"I didn't know that," she said. "Johnny and Jack just disappeared. They returned about three weeks ago. Johnny told me they'd gone to California."

"What else did he tell you?"

"Nothing! Only that they went out there on business."

"What business?"

"I don't know. His poetry, I suppose. But Johnny didn't tell me anything."

Sobers heard the reservation in her voice—*Johnny* hadn't told her anything.

"What did Tracy tell you?"

She squirmed in the chair, caught by her own innate honesty. "He said something about going out there to protect themselves, to protect Johnny's work."

"After they came back, they were here all the time?"

"I don't watch them all the time, Mr. Sobers. Johnny has friends he stays with, places he goes. Jack isn't here always."

"You wouldn't notice if they were gone a few days?"

"I suppose not," she admitted. "But they couldn't have killed anyone, I know that. I know Johnny too well."

"They would have killed me if they could."

"You're wrong! It was some mistake."

"You want to believe that, Mrs. Price."

"All right," she agreed, and put out her cigarette. "Perhaps Johnny never has forgotten his wife or those days all the way. He suffered a great deal from it. But I've lived with him, slept beside him, for five years now, and I know that he isn't bitter about the past anymore."

137

"That isn't how I heard it up there two nights ago," Sobers said. "He looked like a man who could kill Doris and Henry Forbes with his bare hands."

She shook her head. "You're like everyone, Mr. Sobers. You look at his size, his strength, and inside you fear him, think of him as some massive animal. But he's not like that at all. Inside *him* there's only gentleness, compassion, the feelings of a poet for our sad human condition. He doesn't hate his wife anymore, he understands that she was a product of her world. Perhaps I helped him to understand her, I had a husband very much like her."

"Did you send him to prison?" Sobers said.

"Perhaps in my own way I did," she said. "I went back to school, rejected his ambition and success, got my law degree. I refused to be the corporate wife, play the game, so he divorced me. He's a vice-president now, remarried and happy. He still doesn't understand me, but we have a good relation, and I see our children regularly."

"You had to be a person, find yourself," Sobers said.

"No, I knew who I was. I had to lose what I wasn't."

Was that what Susan had done, broken from what she wasn't? He didn't think so, no. Susan hungrier, searching for more.

"I've been lonely often, but that had to be. A clean loneliness, involved in reality and the future, not the numb loneliness of an empty glitter. I found Johnny, he found me. We each have our work, sure in what we're doing, but not always sure in each other. Nothing real is easy. We try to understand each other's needs, struggle with our visions by day, and help each other through the nights. That's why I know Johnny couldn't do what you think. He couldn't hurt anyone, not anymore."

Sobers had heard a lot of people talk about themselves, and most of them were trying to convince themselves how right they were. Elizabeth Price wasn't trying to convince anyone, just explaining the way it was for her. Not sure she was right, but sure of what she was. She had doubts—people without doubts were the blithe destroyers—but she didn't doubt John Glavin. Could he, Sobers, be wrong about the massive poet?

"Not even when he's drunk, Mrs. Price?" Sobers said.

"He can forget his own strength then, yes." Her eyes were dark hollows. "But plan murder? No."

"A man you've lived with for five years returns after a month away and says nothing?"

In the chair she closed her eyes. She sat like some stone statue. "Since he returned he's been drinking—a lot. Lying alone in his room. He hasn't done that in years."

"Something did happen in California?"

Her eyes remained closed. "Jack Tracy spoke of a man named Roy Butler. Cursed him, called him a hungry dog." Her eyes opened. "That's all I know, Mr. Sobers. I love Johnny."

"Have they gone back to California?"

"I think so. The girl came. Johnny wasn't here. She talked to Jack, I heard her mention California. They left together. When Johnny came home, I told him. He went after them."

Sobers walked out. Behind him, Elizabeth Price's voice seemed to speak to the air.

"I love him, but there are more important things."

On Grove Street Sobers waved for another taxi. Had they gone back to San Vicente? To Doris Forbes? And were they two taking one, or three together?

PART THREE

IMAGE IN A DARK WINDOW

17

Two barren mountain chains fill most of Buena Costa County. Inland is the broad expanse of the main Coast Range, and near the sea the spur of the Santa Ysolde Mountains. Steep, rough, and dry, the narrow canyons of the Santa Ysolde reach to the sea and the edge of San Vicente itself. With little water, burned by the hot sun, the canyons are mostly deserted, the domain of chaparral and dusty, twisted live oaks.

Deep in one of the smaller canyons, Gloria Forbes stood on the porch of a rustic cabin, her eyes shining in the fading evening light of the steep canyon. Behind her, John Glavin sat in a rough redwood chair against the cabin wall. It was a ramshackle old cabin, but the broken walls had been recently repaired, and the low roof showed new patches.

"Do you remember this cabin?" Gloria said.

"Part of your grandfather's ranch," Glavin said. "Abandoned a long time ago. Ranching didn't pay out here."

"Peter and I fixed it up in secret. I think mother and

143

Henry forgot we owned it. Our playhouse, Peter's and mine."

"Kids need a hideout, somewhere to explore themselves. Stay a kid as long as you can," Glavin said.

"When are we going to see Doris? That's why we came."

"Soon."

Gloria stared far down the narrow canyon with its brown mesquite and dusty green oaks. "Why didn't you ever come to find me? To talk to me?"

"You were better off with your mother and Forbes. With a dead father."

"That's no answer."

"It'll have to do."

Gloria turned in the fading light. She half-sat against the rickety porch railing looking at the big poet.

"Why did you have to be dead?"

"Maybe to be alive, Gloria."

"Hiding? From mother and Henry? What could they do to you?"

"Maybe it was the other way around. They wouldn't have to worry I'd cause trouble. They could sleep easy."

She turned away again, a small shiver through her full body. She stared down the canyon in the purple twilight.

"Paul Sobers thinks you killed Henry."

"And if I did?"

"Then it was some accident. You had a reason. Something you couldn't help."

Glavin laughed.

"You're my father," Gloria said.

"Do you need a father, girl?"

"Everyone does."

"No matter who he is or what he's done?"

"Yes!" She turned back toward him. "Tell me you killed Susan Sobers, too."

144

"Sure. How about the Kennedys, King, and Che Guevera?"

She looked down at her hands. They were large hands, and she scowled at them. "I don't know what's happening or why, but I know I have to trust you."

"I never met Susan Sobers, Gloria."

"I have to help if I can," she said.

A black car came up the canyon, raising a cloud of yellow dust in the twilight. It turned into the cabin driveway. The driver was a large, swarthy man with a mustache. Jack Tracy sat in the front seat beside the dark man.

"I don't need your help," Glavin said.

He walked down through the heavy chaparral toward the black car. Gloria watched for a moment, then went into the cabin. A telephone stood on an unpainted table. She dialed.

"Peter? I'm back."

"Gloria!" Peter Cole's voice was excited. "We've been—!"

"I'm with my father. He's alive, Peter! I—"

"Your mother's awful worried. The police—"

"Don't tell her, Peter. Not yet. I want to be alone here for a while. I'm out at the cabin with . . . Peter? Hello?"

She held the receiver. The line had gone dead. Then she heard the slow *drag . . . clump . . . drag . . .*

Jack Tracy stood in the open doorway of the cabin. He held the torn telephone wire in his big hand. Behind Tracy, John Glavin leaned against the porch railing, silent.

*

Paul Sobers rented a car in Los Angeles and drove up to San Vicente. It was faster. He reached San Vicente just after 9:00 P.M., and drove straight to the Ruston Clinic. He parked up the dark country road, and walked

145

around the parking lot to the rear of the main building. Tree limbs hung over the high wall that enclosed the rear garden. Sobers went over the wall.

In the shadowed garden under its tall trees, the windows of the first floor rooms sent out shafts of pale light. Sobers didn't know which room Doris Forbes was in, and the first door he tried was locked. He crossed through the garden toward the next door. If it was locked, too, he would have to try to find an open window, and as he moved softly through the garden he looked in at the windows.

Only one window was open. Through it, a man sat in a chair beside the white hospital bed watching television. He was fully dressed in the dim blue light of the TV, and as he turned his head to yawn Sobers saw the Greek-god profile—Roy Butler!

Quickly he slipped to the next back door, counting the room windows as he went. The door was unlocked. He ran into the pale green rear corridor, nearly fell over a medication cart pushed by a startled nurse, bumped an orderly, and began to count the doors along the main corridor.

"Hey! You!"

Two burly men in white ran toward him. He went on counting the doors down the corridor. The two men grabbed him.

"Get the Doc!"

He didn't resist. The door he wanted was three ahead. He kept his eyes on it until Dr. Martin Ruston came scowling along the corridor. Ruston stared in astonishment when he saw Sobers. His smooth face reddened.

"Sobers! Haven't you learned—" Ruston turned on his heel. "The police will—"

"What's Roy Butler doing in your clinic?"

Ruston stopped. "Butler?"

"I want to talk to him. Then I'll see the police."

"You're confusing me, Sobers," the physician-businessman protested. "Are you saying that you think Roy Butler is here in the clinic? If you are, you're quite—"

"I just saw him," Sobers snapped.

"Saw him? Where?"

"In one of the rooms in this corridor. Nice and relaxed, watching TV."

"Which room, damn it!" Ruston exploded, glared along the bright corridor.

Sobers walked ahead to the door he had pinpointed. He turned the knob. The door was locked.

"You lock your rooms? In a hospital?"

"This isn't a hospital, it's a private clinic. Patients come for private reasons, sometimes want privacy. We provide locks and lock the rooms when they are empty. This room is empty, Sobers."

"Where's the key?"

Ruston produced a master key, opened the room door. They went inside. The room was dark and exactly as Sobers had seen it through the window, except that the television was off and the room was empty now. The open window was pushed up higher.

"He was here, Ruston," Sobers said. "Out the window."

Ruston picked up the room telephone, spoke low and sharp. Sobers opened the closet door. A modish, white man's raincoat hung there. Sobers took it out as Ruston put down the phone.

"This room has been unoccupied for a week," Ruston said. "It's reserved for tomorrow—and not for Roy Butler."

"Someone left his raincoat."

"That could have been here for weeks," Ruston said. "You must have seen someone else. A different room."

If the room *hadn't* been empty, Sobers might have believed it, but he had seen someone. He went to the television set. It was still hot.

"Feel it, Ruston," he said.

Ruston felt the set, turned angrily for the door. "I'll see about this! If someone in this clinic let an unauthorized person use this room, I'll know why!"

"Never mind," Sobers said. "He's gone, no one's going to admit anything. I better talk to Doris Forbes. Don't tell me I can't, she could be in a lot of danger."

"She went home two days ago," Ruston said. "Danger?"

Sobers told him about Glavin and Jack Tracy. "Have you seen Gloria, heard that she's back?"

"No," Ruston said. "Her real father *is* alive?"

"And in San Vicente, I think," Sobers said. He had been searching the pockets of the white raincoat and now felt the paper. He pulled it out—a page torn from some pad, with the scribbled address: *Stein Pavilion, Griffith Memorial Hospital, L.A.* Sobers looked up at Ruston. "Is Butler sick, maybe?"

"Not that I've heard," Ruston said.

Sobers put the note into his pocket as he walked out.

*

Dr. Martin Ruston sat in his office behind his desk, the telephone in his hand.

"Sheriff Hoag," he snapped. "When do you expect him? Never mind, give me Lee Beckett." Ruston drummed his fingers on the desk. "Beckett? That Sobers is back! Asking for Mrs. Forbes. I expect you and Hoag to restrain him, you hear?"

Ruston hung up. The door into the next room opened. Roy Butler came into the office, closed the door behind him.

"Next time try to remember your coat," Ruston said.

"I had to move fast."

"Did you hear it all?"

"I heard," Butler said. "Damn that Sobers."

"The police will handle Sobers, we have to find Gloria," Ruston said. "What about this John Glavin and his friend?"

Butler sat on the edge of the desk. He wore a handsome new maroon jacket over slim gray slacks. His pale blue shirt was new, as were his black shoes. He lit a cigarette nervously.

"Maybe we're all wrong about Forbes," he said. "Maybe it was those two."

"I don't care who shot who," Ruston said, "but Sobers seems to think Gloria is with them, and you better look into it."

"Why me?"

"Your interest in Gloria is known, and because of your damned snooping those two already know you. I think it's time you earned your keep, Butler."

"Maybe they tried to kill me already!"

"Then you have an advantage. They can't fool you."

Butler's handsome face was unconvinced. "Or maybe they were really trying to shoot Gloria?"

"I hope not," Ruston said.

Butler stubbed out his cigarette in Ruston's ashtray and stood up. "I wish I really had been with Susan Sobers when she got shot. I might know what else is going on."

"The devil with what's going on. Find Gloria!"

Butler nodded.

*

The big white Forbes house on Mission Ridge was dark. Sobers parked and rang the doorbell. There was no response. No sign of life, not even the housekeeper. Sobers walked around the house toward the garage.

Something moved among the trees. A shadowy figure. Sobers stopped abruptly, turned toward his car in the dark driveway. He had no weapon . . .

The figure stepped out. A female figure in slacks and a sleek suede jacket in the cold night. Lois Butler.

"You've made a bail bondsman happy," she said. "I'm not sure about the sheriff. Was the trip worth it, Paul?"

Her short copper hair was unkempt, as if she hadn't brushed it for days, and her handsome face was drawn, sleepless. Her eyes were too bright, not quite part of the rest of her face.

"Where's Doris Forbes?" Sobers asked.

"I wouldn't know." Indistinct in the night, she seemed to look toward the dark house.

"What are you watching for? Your brother?"

She laughed thinly. "He's probably in Mexico by now."

"No he isn't." He told her what he'd seen at the Ruston Clinic. "Is he sick, Lois?"

She was silent for a time. "What did Ruston say?"

"He denied that Roy was there."

Lois Butler shrugged in the night, said nothing more.

"He was there," Sobers said. "Doris Forbes's first husband, John Glavin, is alive. It looks like he killed Henry, tried to kill Roy. I think he's in town again and maybe still after Roy. Forbes I can understand, revenge. But why shoot Roy? Just because Roy knew he was alive, or is there something else?"

"I'm not Roy's keeper," she said, and looked toward the big house dark in the night. "Revenge? Then maybe Doris—?"

She stopped, and her eyes seemed to blaze in the dark. Sobers watched her.

"You're here to spy on Dr. Taylor," he said.

"Am I?"

"You said that Doris and Taylor weren't having an affair."

"No I didn't. I said I doubted it, and I still do."

"Could we all be wrong about who shot Forbes?"

"Russ?" She laughed again. "For a woman? Never!"

"Is there something he would kill for?"

Lois Butler turned and walked away through the shadowy trees. Sobers heard her car engine start and fade away.

18

The lighted buildings of Newmont College were an oasis in the dark chaparral of the mountains. The stone tower behind the Forbes house loomed high over the college, and the students who walked the lighted paths were neat and serious, with shorter hair and quieter clothes than on the university campuses.

The brown Continental Mark IV stood in the driveway of the president's two-story brown frame house. A young Mexican woman answered Sobers's ring. Behind her, Russell Taylor appeared from an inner room.

"Sobers! This is a surprise. Come in." Taylor nodded to the Mexican girl. "Some coffee please, Rosa."

"If it's hot," the girl said and walked away.

Her voice had no accent and was more than a shade curt.

"Rosa can be difficult," Taylor said, "but she cleans like a demon, cooks like an angel. I'd be lost without her."

"You could learn to cook and clean."

Taylor smiled. "Take care of myself? Completely competent? I'm not sure that would be desirable."

"Why not?"

"Inefficient, Sobers. I can run any college, but I can't do any specific thing that goes on at a college. I can't maintain the buildings, do financial or clerical work, operate a laboratory, or teach any subject except administration if we taught it. And if I had taken the time to learn any of those jobs, it would have been a waste."

"Like the lawyer in *Pinafore* who ran the British Navy but had never been on any ship except a *partner*-ship?"

"You know," Taylor said, "I never found that amusing. A lawyer is probably the best man to head a navy. Any competent lieutenant can operate a ship. Lesser men know how to do things, top men know what must be done and when. A leader hires sailors, professors, and cooks. Rosa is excellent at her work. She likes it. She wouldn't want my work, and if I did hers I'd be wasting my talents."

"Everyone in his place? Then does everyone get the same pay? I mean, if we're all doing our best work."

"Pay is decided by the importance of the job," Taylor said. "That is the law of life, Sobers."

While they talked, Taylor led Sobers into a large library. There were so many books that Taylor had a ladder on wheels to reach the higher shelves. Peter Cole sat at a desk working over plans for some building.

"So," Taylor said. "Does Sheriff Hoag know you're back?"

"I expect he does by now."

"I see. Well, what can I do for you? I have a class to work on with Peter there."

"I thought you didn't teach?"

"A seminar for seniors. Call it 'The President's Pep Talk.' There is a tendency at the universities to tear down our old values. At Newmont we try to teach what made America great."

Peter Cole looked up. "Dr. Taylor says a student is an apprentice to life, needs to know our beliefs as well as our knowledge. We believe that the world prospers on individual ambition, everyone trying to get everything."

Sobers knew where Peter Cole got his solemn ways—the protégé walking in the footsteps of his teacher.

"Most of us never get near everything," Sobers said.

"The best men get more, yes," Taylor agreed, "but the average man gets his share and is content. We must never hamper the strong to protect the weak, or we all lose."

"Nice for the strong," Sobers said. "Right now I want to talk to Doris Forbes. Where is she? Has Gloria come home?"

"Gloria? Not that I've heard," Taylor said. "Doris is at home, as far as I know. Just up the road from us."

Peter Cole said, "I thought Gloria was away looking for her father?"

"She found him." Sobers told them about John Glavin and Tracy. "Now I think they're in San Vicente, they probably have Gloria with them, and I didn't get any answer at the Forbes house. It's totally dark, not even the housekeeper there."

"Gloria's father is dangerous?" Peter Cole said.

"The housekeeper's away for a week," Taylor said, "but Doris should be there. I spoke to her this morning, she said she would be at home tonight. Let's go and see!"

*

Lois Butler closed the motel room door.

"So you didn't leave town. Why not tell me?"

She sat down on the bed, glared at her brother.

"How'd you find me?" Roy Butler said.

"Once that Sobers said he'd seen you at Ruston's clinic it wasn't hard. People owe a lawyer favors. You were supposed to leave town after Gloria was shot and Forbes died."

154

"I changed my mind."

"You don't have a mind to change! Gloria's not going to marry you now or ever, you idiot."

"That doesn't matter anymore. A whole new ball game, sis." Butler's furtive eyes were eager in the motel room. "I've got a lot better than Gloria. Once we find her—"

"We?"

Roy grinned. "Like I said, sis, I'm in at the top. Real this time, no more schemes. This is my chance."

"You're a fool!"

The handsome con-man's eyes turned muddy. "Yeh? Well you don't know a damn thing about it! I tell you it's cold, everything nice and smooth. They've got to cut me in. With what I know—"

"Know?" Lois watched him. "What do you know?"

"Never mind," Roy said, smug. "It'll make me big."

"It'll make you dead! Twice you've been shot at. If it wasn't Henry Forbes, the killer's still loose!"

Butler's eyes jumped, but his handsome face set as firmly as it could. He looked at his sister stubbornly. Her gaze was stronger than his, and his eyes lowered.

"Once," he said. "I don't know what happened to Susan Sobers. That was just to help close it all up fast. Maybe it wasn't even once. Gloria could have been the target after all."

"You lied?" Lois was up in the small room. "You mean you weren't with the Sobers woman? Then anyone could have—"

Roy turned away, began to pace. "I'm going to grab this chance! It's all swell for you. You're educated, you've got what you need to be someone! What have I got? Where do I get a new start? A never-was dropout! Who gives me a career? I'm lucky if I get hired as a messenger with the old men and the half-wits! I want

155

what everyone wants and not damn many get! A winner, not a loser!'"

"You'll get a slab in the morgue!" She stepped closer to him, touched his arm. "Roy, please, we'll work something out—"

"No!" He pulled away. Then he grinned. "Hey, I can take care of myself, sis. I'm a big boy now."

"Yes, I suppose you are."

He went on grinning. "It's my chance, Lo. The big one."

"All right, Roy." She smiled at him.

*

Russell Taylor hammered on the door of the dark Forbes house.

"Doris? It's Russ. I know you're in there. Doris!"

There was the rumble of traffic far below on the freeway, and something small scurried through the chaparral. Then light steps approached the door inside. Hesitant steps.

"Russ?" Doris Forbes's voice, soft and low.

"Yes! Sobers is with me. He's found John Glavin alive!"

The door opened. She stood in the dark entrance hall, her hand to her face, and her eyes looking past Taylor and Sobers as they went in. She closed the door quickly.

"Someone's been watching the house, Russ! Off and on all day! Out there among the trees."

"Why didn't you call for help?" Sobers said.

"I wasn't sure until it got dark and I saw him still out there! I did call Russ once, but he wasn't home, and I didn't want to be just a jittery old woman. After it got dark I was afraid to turn on the lights or make a call. I'm here alone, he could have been listening! If I didn't do anything, perhaps he wouldn't know I was here. There could even be more than one. I thought I saw a man and

156

a woman out there earlier."

"No, that was me and Lois Butler," Sobers said.

"Lois?" Taylor said. "Outside this house?"

"Maybe we were the only ones you saw?" Sobers said.

"Were you still out there twenty minutes ago?" Doris said.

"No."

"Then there's someone else."

Taylor went to the front window. "I don't see anyone now. We need some light. Let him know Doris isn't alone."

Sobers turned on the lights. Doris Forbes stood pale in the high-ceilinged living room. She wore a long purple lounging robe and her voice shook:

"I'm afraid, Russ. Out there in the dark. Who is he? What does he want?"

She sat down in the old living room of the big house, her hands tight on the arms of her chair. Russell Taylor stood over her, protective yet uneasy, like a man out of his element, wishing he were back tending to business he could control.

"Glavin's alive, Doris," Sobers said. "He's living in New York, but he was out here when Henry and Gloria were shot, and he's back out here now."

"You think he's the one watching this house?" Taylor said.

"I don't know," Sobers said. "Has Gloria been in touch with you, Doris?"

Doris Forbes had said nothing when Sobers announced that he had found John Glavin. Her high-boned face was remote with a kind of distant sadness.

"Gloria? No, not since she went away again," she said, almost unconcerned. "What is he like, Paul? What is he doing?"

"I told you once about a man Gloria had met—Frank

Kapek? Glavin is Frank Kapek. Bearded, scarred, like an overage hippie. A hippie-poet writing in New York and living with a woman who's a lot like he is. Working to teach the world the truth."

She almost smiled. "So he hasn't changed at all? The way he should have been without me. I'm glad."

"He's changed," Sobers said. "He's a drunk, he's violent, and he's probably sick in his head. He's here with a friend as violent as he is and maybe sick, too. I think he, or they, shot Henry and Gloria, and now—"

"Sick?" She was seeing another time and place. "Because he married me. He paid a big price for that mistake."

"Damn it," Taylor swore, "he was probably crazy always! I know his kind. Misfits, whining failures dragging the whole country down! They think that because no one wants their 'art' it must be pure, beautiful! But it's only useless, and so are they! I have only contempt for his kind. Weak and crazy!"

"Crazy, maybe," Sobers said, "but not weak. Men like Glavin lead a hard life; they're tough."

"Even when they don't go to prison," Doris said.

"He went to prison because he couldn't face reality!" Taylor said, angry. "Your marriage was a mistake, but he wouldn't face that, so killed a man. It's not hard to evade reality, indulge your own ego. Men like him are afraid to measure up in the real world, hide in illusions. My father was a two-bit salesman. I went to a Bible-belt college and got my doctorate at night. I was a mediocre student, but I got ahead while the brilliant boys were dreaming. I took dog jobs, ran errands, made myself *needed*. I never took a job that wasn't a step ahead. I learned my trade, and now I'm a valuable man. I've earned success."

Doris Forbes looked up at Taylor. "Yes, you're strong,

158

Russ. Johnny never was—"

"Damn it, don't be a fool, Doris! Glavin is dirty, crazy and dangerous. Sobers thinks—"

"I . . . I hurt him, Russ. Whatever he's done, I owe him his new—"

"You owe him nothing. You owe no one anything," Taylor said. He touched her shoulder, his eyes hard. "It's time we stopped being scared. Henry's dead, you're free, and John Glavin isn't going to hurt us. I'm here, and I'm going to stay. Us, Doris. I'm going to the police and they'll stop that madman, and then we'll go on all the way."

Taylor bent and kissed her. He looked defiantly at Sobers and strode from the room and out of the big old house.

*

Peter Cole drove his small Ford out of San Vicente and into the mountains that ringed the city. He drove through the dark night and turned into a narrow canyon.

The mountain road was like a tunnel in the headlights, the road and the steep canyon as silent and remote as Mars. But behind and below, the lights of San Vicente seemed close enough to reach out and touch.

Peter Cole didn't look at the dazzling view. He drove on, and when the light of a cabin showed faintly through the twisted oaks and mesquite, he slowed. He reached a sharp curve, switched off the headlights, and drove slowly on around the curve to park facing ahead in the night.

The cabin stood on a rise a hundred yards up the road. Light showed in its windows and open doorway. A woman came out onto the cabin porch, stood at the porch railing. Peter Cole leaned forward in his car, peering through the night.

Behind the woman, the hulking figure of a man came

159

out. Another figure stood in the cabin doorway, grotesque against the light, like a small child with the head and shoulders of a man.

Peter Cole sat rigid with his hands on the steering wheel. His knuckles were white, bloodless. The woman and the big man went back into the cabin. The door closed. Peter Cole sat in his car for some time, staring ahead at the closed cabin door.

Then he started the car and drove back the way he had come. He came out of the narrow canyon, circled San Vicente on back roads, and when he reached the freeway he turned south toward Los Angeles.

19

Alone in the bright living room of the big house with Doris Forbes, Sobers sensed the night they'd had together in Marin County rising warm and heavy between them.

"So it *is* you and Taylor?"

Her blonde hair and fine-boned face stood out against the purple robe. She no longer gripped the arms of her chair, as if her tension had gone with Taylor, or, alone with Sobers, she was no longer afraid.

"I'm too dependent on men, Paul. Russ has ideas about us; he assumes I have the same ideas."

"Do you?"

"I'm alone now. I need someone."

"I guess we both do," Sobers said.

Her face was half turned away from him, one delicate hand shading her eyes in the bright room. Small under the purple robe, she shifted in the chair.

"I feel like a pale old hag. Turn off some of that light." She smiled. "I'm a vain woman, Paul. Or are *vain* and *woman* synonymous?"

Sobers turned off all but one table lamp, sat down

facing her across the now muted room. Outside, the night seemed closer.

"How are you feeling really?" he asked.

"There's nothing wrong with me some make-up, a dazzling new dress, and a long vacation wouldn't cure." She shook her head and sighed. "A long, long vacation away from everything. Suddenly I feel stripped and nameless. Like an unknown and unnoticed child."

"Weren't you noticed as a child?"

"Not often."

She seemed to think about her childhood. The shadows of the now dim room etching her aristocratic face and the outline of her body under the robe. Watching her, Sobers tried to imagine her with John Glavin. He couldn't. Blunt and simple, even crude, Glavin didn't seem to fit with her at all. Maybe he'd been different then, young and unsure, dazzled by her difference. Or perhaps she had been different, younger and simpler, the rounder girl he had seen under her polish.

"It isn't over, is it?" she said. "When can we start to forget?"

"Is that what you want? To forget it all? Call it over? Your husband, Henry, tried to shoot Roy Butler, shot Gloria instead—thought he'd killed her, so killed himself? You want to leave it at that, we all go home? Henry Forbes tried to kill Butler because he'd been your lover?"

She watched him. "I told you I'd had other men."

"You didn't tell me Butler was one of them. That changes things, gives you a different relation to Butler."

"I have some pride! A cheap male animal like him. We pay for our little hungers, don't we? He flattered me. Younger, handsome, eager. Stupid, stupid! So many mistakes we never mean and that we have to lie in the dark with. All that handsome, shiny flesh to take me, even if it was hollow!"

162

"You're sure it's over? On both sides?"

"You think I might have been jealous of Gloria?"

"When I met Lois Butler outside this house tonight, I asked her if she was waiting for Roy. She didn't act at all surprised that I'd think Butler could be here."

"I can't help what Lois Butler might think! If Roy did come here, it wouldn't be for love!"

"What would it be for?"

"Nothing!" Her eyes flashed in the dim room. "And if Lois Butler was watching this house, it wasn't for her brother. She's probably spying on Russ Taylor, hounding him."

"You said there's nothing between you and Taylor."

"I said not on my side and not yet. Who can say about the future, and I can't help it if he wants me. But until now anything more than close friends was all in his mind."

"How much in his mind?"

"You mean—?" Her peal of laughter filled the muted room. "Murder for a woman? Russ? Never!"

"You and Lois agree on that at least."

"Do we really?"

Suddenly Sobers found her eyes looking past him again, the way they had the first time they'd met. He didn't have to turn to know that she was seeing her image in the dark windows.

"Aren't you worried about Gloria?" he said. "Where she is, who she could be with?"

"Yes, I'm worried. But, you know, if all this has done nothing else, it's made me realize that she's grown up. She's a woman, isn't she? I can't dictate to her any more, can't control her life." She shook her head, half sadly, half smiling. "It's a strange feeling, Paul. So many years."

"They pass," he said. "You've changed, you know?"

163

She wasn't the same woman he'd met in this room that first day. That woman had been sleek and manufactured, as crisp and brittle as a plastic doll, arranged and assured, dominating her husband and daughter. All that was gone from the woman in the robe, with her blonde hair loose, the hollows of her face like shadows in the low light.

"Mrs. Henry Forbes," she said. "In her small, sure world. A husband away too much, but that was fine. A proper daughter at home. Polite gentlemen friends and a few sweaty skeletons. Brisk, safe, nicely busy. When did it change?"

"When Forbes died."

"Reality?" She held her arms out. "Paul?"

He went to her, and she kissed him. He felt her body naked under the purple robe, alive and light. She was there to be taken again, but Sobers felt the resistance inside himself. Something in him resisted. Unanswered questions? Who was she, what did she want? A lot like Susan, nothing like Gloria. Mother and daughter—and Doris his own age, his own kind, but so much like Susan. And who and what had Susan been for him? Unknown shadows looming between . . .

She screamed.

Up, he almost fell and saw it for only a second—a ghostly face at the window behind him. Like a severed head on a plate, mouth open, and gone.

He ran into the hall and out the front door. The window was at the front of the house. No one was there. In the night, nothing moved among the trees. Then a car started somewhere up the road, and faded away.

*

Russell Taylor didn't look at the old man on his library couch. Taylor made a scotch and water at the liquor cabinet.

"Drink?" he asked.

164

"I helped myself while I waited," Otto Genseric said.

The president of Calixco Petroleum leaned back on the couch. A soft gray Stetson on his silver hair, the late Henry Forbes's boss wore his trademark combination of western boots and conservative business suit. One rough hand rubbed slowly over his pink face, and he didn't seem happy.

"Time's wasting," he said.

"I'm as anxious as you are," Russell Taylor said. He took a long drink, and went to sit at his desk. "That Paul Sobers is snooping around again. The police will stop him, but now—"

"Your problems don't interest me," Genseric said. "Time does. At my age, Taylor, you don't postpone picking an apple, you eat it now. My contacts are in the right places now, not tomorrow. Power is a delicate balance, timing is everything."

"I know, damn it," Taylor snapped. "I think Gloria is back in town. We'll find her and finish up. Sobers thinks she may be with Doris's first husband. It seems he's alive after all, was probably behind all the trouble we've run into."

"That isn't my problem either."

"What is your problem?" Taylor said irritably. "In addition to the hand of time, that is."

Genseric smiled. "Very little. An advantage of having a great deal of money other people would like a share in. But the delays are beginning to annoy me. First Henry Forbes and that Roy Butler; now Gloria's whims. I suggest you reach her soon. I can go elsewhere, eh?"

Russell Taylor finished his drink.

*

Sobers returned to the living room. "No one there, and the ground's too hard to show footprints. But I heard a car up the road."

165

"Johnny?" Doris said.

"Probably. Tracy couldn't move that fast."

"Johnny killed Henry, shot everyone?" She took a cigarette from a jade box on the table beside her chair. "You think he wants to kill me, too, don't you?"

"Don't you?" Sobers said. He sat down again, his long body awkward in the narrow chair. "That was another thing you forgot to tell me—how you met and married Henry Forbes."

"It wasn't your business," she said. She smoothed the robe over her thighs. "Yes, Henry was the prosecutor against Johnny. We fell in love. When I moved down here, Henry took the job with Calixco to join me. When my father-in-law died, we were married. Was that so awful?"

"Not to me, and not if that's all that happened."

"It's all that happened."

"Roy Butler dug it up and told Gloria. He also told her that Glavin might still be alive. It was enough to send her searching for Glavin, but is it enough for revenge? Murder?"

"I hope it isn't. I hope you're wrong about Johnny."

"Maybe I am." He watched her. "You knew about yourself and Butler, about Gloria and the past, before Forbes was shot. Yet you insisted that Forbes couldn't have killed himself, had no reason."

She nodded. "I was lying, yes. I thought of Johnny and the past at once. Henry had never stopped feeling guilty. A shadow over him, looking behind him for a ghost, and it seemed to get worse every year no matter how much I told him he had no reason for guilt. If anyone had injured Johnny unfairly, it was me. All that did was make him withdraw from me."

"So you turned to other men."

"We came together through a tragedy, and when that

tragedy broke him, all I could do was go to other men. Pretty, yes?"

"Don't wallow, it's too easy. You had a husband ruining himself with guilt, so you turned to other men. Most women would do the same—and most men, too."

"Would they?" she said, smoked. "I thought that Henry's guilt had finally broken him, but I still wanted to keep it all from Gloria, so I lied that night, insisted it had to be murder. But then Peter Cole told me Gloria had gone off alone, and I realized she wasn't eloping, that she must know about Johnny. There was no more reason to hide the past or what it had done to Henry. It was obvious what had happened."

"Glavin was dead, so it had to be Forbes," Sobers said. "But now Glavin's alive. He was here with ⸢ ʳacy when Forbes, Gloria, and my wife were shot."

Her wide, warm eyes looked past Sobers once more, looked at the dark windows as she smoked. Unblinking, she looked at her own image staring back at her.

"Could you be wrong, Paul? About Johnny?"

"You want it to be Forbes? Close it up and forget it? *Hope* that Glavin won't kill you, too?"

"I can't see him hurt again! I—"

"Can you see Gloria hurt?"

She stiffened. "Gloria?"

"I think she's with Glavin, here in San Vicente. I don't know why, or how he feels about her. I don't know if she's a prisoner or a partner."

She sat as if paralyzed. Sobers shifted his long body in the small chair and listened to the silence of the old house.

"I won't ask you or the police not to hurt Johnny," she said at last. "If he's dangerous, you must protect yourselves. But—"

"It could still be something else," Sobers said. "Why

167

did Roy Butler dig up the past in the first place? And if Glavin killed Forbes, why did he go back to New York without taking a shot at you then? There could be some other answer."

She shook her head. "What other answer?"

"Someone could be using Glavin. Someone who knew he was alive, knew where he was. Someone who knew that if Forbes was shot, Glavin would be the first suspect as soon as it became known that he was alive."

"My God, Paul—!"

Her face was incredulous, and then a sudden cough made them both turn. Lee Beckett was in the room doorway.

"You might make a good cop, Sobers," Beckett said. "It's a pretty devious theory and not bad."

The gray-haired county investigator came into the room.

"Who called you?" Sobers said. "Dr. Ruston?"

"Everyone." Beckett turned to Doris. "Russell Taylor told us about someone watching this house and about your first husband. We'll put a man outside while we look for Glavin."

"Never mind me, find my daughter!" She told Beckett what Sobers had said about Gloria.

"We'll find her," Beckett said. "Sobers? Let's go."

"Beckett, listen! I'll surrender, but first—"

"Shut up!" Beckett glared at him. "We've got a fugitive warrant, the book. I warned you, damn it!" He went on glaring at Sobers. "The sheriff'll throw away the key!"

Sobers said nothing. Beckett still glared at him.

"He's that sure," the investigator said, "but I'm not, so I haven't reported you yet. I'll hold off one more time. That wound on your head, and one other thing, makes me think this case isn't solved yet. I want the truth."

"What other thing?" Sobers said.

"San Rafael called. Kincaid found that woman you had them look for, Sandra Innes. Dead."

20

Lieutenant Kincaid said, "She was in a ravine near Nogales. Shot twice with a .32-caliber pistol the night she disappeared. It was the same gun that shot Gloria Forbes in the Redwood Motel."

They were in the San Rafael morgue. It was the small hours of morning in the nothern California city. Sandra Innes lay naked in the morgue drawer. Taller than her sister, prettier even now, but with the tracks of time in the loose skin of her thighs and belly. Lee Beckett and Sobers stood looking at the body. The sister, Maxine Innes, sat in a corner of the morgue like a bundle of old clothes.

"All her life she got phone calls, went out," Maxine Innes said to no one in particular. "They called, she went. I told her. I said, 'Sandra, someday . . .' But they called, and she went. Always her, never me."

"You were lucky," Kincaid said.

Maxine Innes didn't look like someone who thought she was lucky. As if she'd rather have had the late night calls and be lying dead in a morgue than living in a

170

backwater town with no night calls in her past or her future.

"What did you find at the scene?" Beckett asked.

"Nothing. She was dressed, no rape. Her purse had ten bucks in it, nothing missing. No marks on her except the bullets in the chest and head. No evidence except the shell casings—nothing in her car, no tracks."

"Can I talk to the sister?" Sobers said.

"Go ahead."

He found a chair, sat facing Maxine Innes. She looked at him as if the last thing in the world she cared about was what he might want from her.

"Maxine," Sobers said, "when I talked to you about John Glavin, told you he might be alive, you reacted. Why?"

"I don't know nothin' about John Glavin!"

"Sandra's dead, Maxine. Shot. By someone she knew well enough to meet alone at night. Not a date, she said she'd be back in an hour, but important enough to make her go. What?"

"Money maybe. That'd do it."

"Or fear?" Sobers waited, but Maxine Innes didn't respond. "Maxine, you'll only protect who killed her."

"Who said I was protecting anyone!"

Sobers said, "John Glavin *is* alive. I think he killed Henry Forbes, killed another woman, tried to kill a man named Roy Butler, and shot his own daughter. He probably killed Sandra, but the police have to prove it. They have to prove it and stop him before he kills again."

Her eyes flickered toward her dead sister. Toward Kincaid. Toward the corners of the room. Everywhere except at Sobers. She rubbed at a stain on her shabby cardigan.

"There was a guy named Butler a couple or three

months ago. He talked to Sandra. I don't know what he wanted, but that day she had extra money, you know?"

"They talked about the Glavin case?" Beckett asked.

"All I know is she got extra money," Maxine said. "Then there was someone else. Maybe six, seven weeks ago. In a car out front. Sandra went off a while. It shook her."

"What kind of car?" Sobers said. "A green wagon?"

"Could've been. I don't remember clear."

"Did you see Butler or the car again?" Kincaid asked.

"No." She squirmed. "But there was a phone call. Long distance from around L.A. . . . . a couple of weeks later. She took it in the bedroom."

"About a month ago?" Sobers said.

Maxine Innes nodded.

"You remember the shooting at the Redwood Motel? Was the call around then? A day or so before, maybe?"

"Ain't much happens in Nogales. The call was the same night. I remember I wondered some."

"The same night?" Sobers frowned. "What time?"

"Eight, nine o'clock."

"The evening of the eleventh, *after* the shooting?" Kincaid said. "Or the evening of the tenth, *before* the shooting?"

"Tenth, before the ruckus at the Redwood."

"So the caller wasn't the shooter," Kincaid said.

Sobers nodded, but he was studying Maxine Innes as if he had just seen something hidden deep inside the sister.

"Maxine? When I accused John Glavin of wanting revenge on his wife and Henry Forbes for marrying and stealing his inheritance, he said 'Wife and property. That too.' What do you think he meant by 'that too?' What else did they do?"

"They sent him to jail, ain't that enough?"

172

"Maybe," Sobers said. "You said that when Sandra got money from Roy Butler, it was 'extra' money. Extra to what? What money did she get regularly? From where? Pension? Stocks?"

Maxine Innes said nothing. She looked away.

"We can check her bank," Kincaid said.

"Blackmail, Sobers?" Beckett said.

"Maxine?" Sobers said.

She only glowered up at them.

"She's dead, Maxine," Sobers said. "It's all over, except catching who killed her. Who was paying her? How long?"

"Eighteen years. A few lousy bucks a month, that's all," Maxine said. "Unger was dead. She'd put a lot of years into him, a lot of plans. She was owed!"

"Who?" Beckett said. "For what?"

"I don't know exactly. She never said."

"I think I do," Sobers said. "Who and what."

*

Outside the cabin in its narrow canyon, the dawn light turned the mountains and the gnarled oaks and thick brush a pale gold. Birds greeted the return of light.

"I want to go outside," Gloria Forbes said.

"When Johnny gets back," Jack Tracy said.

The dwarf-like old man sat on the cabin floor near the door, his back against the wall, his elephant shoes out in front of him. He was reading—a literary review—swearing at the review of a book of poems.

"They don't know good poetry from crap. This jerk he likes junk! What do they know about great? Nothin'!"

"You think I'll run off, and you couldn't stop me."

"Johnny'll be back soon, kid."

"I can't leave, can I? Go home."

"You wouldn't want to leave your old man, would you?"

Tracy grinned at the girl. His small eyes were hard and black. He had no visible weapon, but a bulge under his shabby suit jacket showed where a pistol was thrust into his belt. He went on reading, muttering at the fools who praised mediocrity.

"That car last night," Gloria said. "I thought it was Peter. You and my father didn't want him to see me."

"He saw you," Tracy said. "Only he saw us, too."

"Then it couldn't have been Peter. Or Paul Sobers."

"You like that Sobers guy?"

Gloria had been lying on the narrow cabin cot. Now she sat up. Tracy moved his hand toward his belt. Gloria watched him.

"What are you to my father? Why are you with him?"

"Friends, kid. Real friends. You wouldn't know, you never been in the joint. Inside, a friend is all you got, everything. No family, no kids, no wife, just a friend."

"I think you live off him. Like a tapeworm, a parasite."

"He needs me!"

"I think he's afraid of you," she said. "I've watched him, and he's afraid of you, worried. Was he always, or is it now?"

"Shut up!" Tracy controlled rage. "Johnny ain't afraid. We're a team. People better be afraid, stay out of our way." Rage welling up, he flung the magazine across the room. The act seemed to vent the rage, his voice suddenly calmed. "He's a great poet, Johnny. The world needs him. He got to do his work, write, tell it true. I got to protect him, manage him, you see? I got to make people hear him. A team. John Glavin and Jack Tracy. The world, it's gonna remember us!"

"Is that what he's doing now?" Gloria said. "Getting some people out of your way? Roy Butler? Paul Sobers? My mother? Has he gone to kill them? Will he kill me, too?"

174

"Would a guy kill his own kid?" Tracy said. He smiled.

"No, but you would, and I'm not sure my father could stop you. I think you're insane."

Tracy stopped smiling. "You don't say that!"

"Insane, and maybe you've made him insane. Made him hate, want revenge. For what? Because my mother met a man at the trial and married him? Because my grandfather—"

"What do you know!"

"I know. Roy Butler told me. But only an insane—"

"Shut up!" Tracy breathed hard. "You want to know? All of it?"

"Butler told me all about—"

"Shut up!" The legless old man's eyes were black and bright. "Johnny's wife and Unger were lovers, right? Wrong! Johnny was set up. All a fake. That one night. They set Johnny up to kill Unger—and after they paid Unger's woman to lie, to say that Unger and your old lady was in a long affair."

"Set up?" Gloria stood up. "They?"

"Forbes and your old lady. She was screwin' around all right, but with Forbes! Down in Frisco, up in Marin, and way before the trial or the killin'. She wanted out, but she wanted to keep Johnny's inheritance! So they set it up for Johnny to find her with Unger, made sure he was dead drunk, goaded him into the fight, and paid off Unger's woman to lie. A frame all the way, kid, all the way!"

Gloria Forbes sat down. She put her hand to her mouth as if to stifle a sound. But she made no sound.

*

Beckett and Sobers reached San Vicente again in mid-morning. The day was growing hot as they hurried to their cars.

175

"I'll lay it out to Hoag," Beckett said. "We'll blanket the county for Glavin and Tracy."

"I'll talk to Doris Forbes," Sobers said.

"Stay out of trouble. I'll try to get the fugitive warrant dropped. And for God's sake lay off Ruston. If you dig up anything on Glavin—*call!*"

Sobers nodded and drove once more up to Mission Ridge. The Forbes house stood oddly silent again, as if it were one of the victims of the violence sweeping around it.

Sobers rang. The footsteps that approached the door inside were neither slow nor light, and it opened abruptly. Lois Butler stood there with angry eyes.

"I want—!" She didn't go on. Sobers wasn't who she had expected to see.

"You should pay rent, Lois," Sobers said.

She walked away without another word. Sobers followed her into the living room of the big white house. She took a cigarette from Doris's jade box, lit it, and turned to face Sobers, anger in every fiber but saying nothing.

"Where's Doris?" he asked.

"Not here, obviously."

"Shadowing Taylor again?"

Bare-shouldered in a black halter-dress with a full peasant skirt, there was a feeling of tension only barely covered by her anger. She tried to cover it with a shrug.

"Not shadowing, bearding. I came to lay it out, as they say. Find out the lady's intentions."

"Meaning you know the gentleman's intentions?"

"He's seeing a bit too much of her in the open these days. Not even the courtesy to sneak and hide. Well, she's free now; I guess he can have her if he wants her."

"That's what you came to tell her?"

"I came to find out if she wants him."

176

"You think she'll tell you?"

She shrugged again. "Maybe you know? You're around her a lot, too. Maybe you have some ideas about her."

"It's not my ideas she has to worry about right now," he said. "Roy told Gloria about how her father went to prison eighteen years ago, Lois. I wonder if he told her all he knew?"

She had her own problem. "What do men see in her? What does Doris have that's so special?"

"Vulnerability, interest," Sobers said. "Roy wouldn't try a little blackmail, would he?"

"Roy?" She shook her head. Both hands rested on the spread of her hips, as if feeling, measuring. "What can she offer that I can't? What better than this?"

In a single motion she raised her full skirt up above her waist. She wore only sheer panty-hose that shaped her curved hips and long thighs and hid nothing of her flat belly and the dark mound beneath. She had a beautiful body, and Sobers felt his reaction down to his toes. He hid it. Her eyes didn't match the provocation of the gesture.

"Nothing. Only she doesn't display it," he said. "I thought we were supposed to be outgrowing the Stone Age?"

She let the skirt drop, stubbed out her cigarette, and walked out. It was some time before Sobers heard her car start up the road and drive off.

In the living room he took his own cigarette from the jade box. Was she feeling rejected because Taylor seemed to be after Doris? Or was that only what she wanted him to think?

He went out to the garage. The red Mercedes was gone.

Back in the house he called Russell Taylor. The Mexican girl, Rosa, answered. Dr. Taylor wasn't there. Mrs. Forbes wasn't there. Peter Cole wasn't there. She did not know where anyone was except Peter Cole, who was with his family in Jackson Wells, as she had told Mrs. Forbes earlier.

"Where is Jackson Wells?"

"Beyond the mountains. Other side of the county."

Sobers went out to his car and drove to the first gas station below Mission Ridge to ask directions to Jackson Wells.

21

The southeastern corner of Buena Costa County, the district of Jackson Wells, is a high desert plateau eroded in violent reds and yellows. South the desert fades into the greener land of the next county, and, eventually, there is Los Angeles. North, east, and west, the desert is ringed by mountains.

Two secondary highways join the dusty desert city of Jackson Wells itself to the rest of the state and county. One, from the east, ends in the small city. The other comes up from the south, passes through the wide town square, and continues on north to cross the Coast Range at Mesa Grande Pass into Monteverde, the second city of Buena Costa County. There is no direct road to the coast and San Vicente, and it is easier to drive to Jackson Wells from Los Angeles than from San Vicente.

There is a feeder airline from San Vicente to Jackson Wells, and Sobers caught the noon flight. The high-winged Otter skimmed the mountains to Jackson Wells in half an hour. He rented a car, drove through the city with its low buildings, unpaved side streets, and wide town square to another gas station. They gave him directions to "the Cole place."

A dark sky threatened over the desert where even the dry mesquite struggled to survive, and the winter wind blew gritty dust. Still Indian country, the yellow cliffs and flat brown mesas loomed without a blade of grass except where the ranchers had dammed the sparse water. Through a wagon-wheel archway, the Cole ranch was a barn and corral, a bunkhouse, and a main house in good repair among a few scraggly trees beside a stagnant pond. For this part of Buena Costa County, where Indians still died of malnutrition up in High Creek, it was a decent spread. The only car Sobers saw was a battered pickup.

He got no answer to his knocking, but as he turned to walk around the house, he heard a creaking noise from inside. He tried the door, found it open, and went into a low ranchhouse living room with dark ceiling beams, a blackened adobe fireplace, and incongruous plastic, department-store furniture. The creaking came from behind a door across the living room.

It was a small, bare bedroom. An old man sat in a rocker in front of the rear window. He was rocking and staring out at the bleak view of yellow-gray land, barren mesas, and distant black mountains. He didn't stop rocking or turn.

"My son's in town," he said. "Running his business."

He was too old to be Peter Cole's father.

"Where's Peter?"

"Peter?" The old man watched the distant land. "He used to like the land, Peter. My son sent him away to learn how to make money. No time for the land."

"But he's here now?"

"You got to live *in* this land, not on it."

"You've lived here a long time?"

"Long?" He seemed to think about time. "Came with

180

my father, raised cattle. My son takes care of me. He runs a fleet of trucks, makes money. He doesn't know the land."

"It's your land then," Sobers said.

"No one's land," the old man said. "Cattle don't pay. We done something wrong. Don't know what."

The old man went on staring out at the vast desert under the heavy black sky. Sobers watched him, and outside he heard a car bounce along the road and stop at the house. He went out into the old living room with its new furniture. Peter Cole came in the front door. He saw Sobers, stopped dead.

"Mr. Sobers!" He looked around. "You're alone?"

He wore an old denim jacket, boot jeans, and boots. He seemed at ease in the old clothes, as if they had a kind of inner comfort, familiar. But his eyes weren't at ease.

"I'm alone," Sobers said. "Are you?"

"Me? Yes, of course. Can I . . . Can I get you a drink?"

Peter crossed the living room to another door, went into a small study–sitting room. He stood at a cabinet. The walls of the room were covered with enlarged photographs of the desert and mesas, of seamed Indian faces and the wrinkled eyes of ranchers under low Stetson brims. Good photos, the work of a craftsman, even an artist. A long table was piled with cameras, an enlarger, and materials.

"No drink," Sobers said. "Are those your work?"

Peter looked at the photos. "Yes."

"They're damned good."

"I don't do it much anymore."

"Why?"

Peter left the cabinet, sat down. "Dr. Taylor says it's a waste of my time. He says pictures aren't real because there isn't any concrete reality—only what you make people think is real. Besides, he hates people who work alone on some private idea. You've got to work in the outside world as it is."

"It's still good work to me," Sobers said. "You came home for a little vacation?"

"I like to come home sometimes."

"Funny time. With Gloria still not back, all that."

"Yes, well..." Peter was nervous. "I wanted to think."

"About Gloria?"

"About myself, I guess. Gloria hasn't exactly been rushing back to me, and Dr. Taylor—"

The car that now came along the ranch road outside had a foreign motor. Peter Cole cocked his head to listen. Sobers didn't. He knew who it would be.

"What about Dr. Taylor?" he said.

Peter shook his head. "I don't know, he's been distracted. Too busy to work on things with me."

The car stopped outside. Peter went out into the living room. Sobers waited in the study. He watched Peter open the front door, saw Doris Forbes hurry inside.

"Is she here, Peter?" She wore a tailored black jump suit, her blonde hair blown by the wind of the long drive from San Vicente. "Gloria, I mean?"

"No, Mrs. Forbes," Peter said.

She sat down. "When I heard that you'd come here, I thought perhaps... I called, but some old man answered and didn't make much sense, so I ..." She sighed, took out a cigarette. "Well, I had to do something more than sit around."

Sobers came from the study. "I'm here, Doris."

"Paul! How did ... ? Ah, you flew! You *would* make a good policeman."

"Not patient enough. Nothing from Gloria at all?"

"No. When Rosa told me Peter had gone home, I had the wild hunch Gloria would be here."

"Peter came to think. Taylor's been too busy."

"Trying to help me, yes." She held her unlit cigarette. "What is she doing, Paul?"

"Peter?" Sobers said. "In New York I had the thought that our search might be a charade. That maybe Gloria already knew that Glavin was alive and who he was. That she was just using me to find him again. Did she ever say anything about that?"

"No," Peter said. "Nothing."

Doris said, "You can't think Gloria and Johnny—!"

"Mrs. Forbes?" Peter said. "What about your house?"

"House?" Sobers said.

"He means an offer we've had for the Mission Ridge property," Doris explained. "We get offers every few years, but Gloria has never really thought of selling."

"Gloria?" Sobers said.

"Yes, the houses are in her name. Johnny's father left them that way. In my trust until she's twenty-one."

"How much was the offer?"

"The market value, no more. Two hundred and fifty thousand, nothing special, and Gloria isn't of age even if she wanted—"

"But Glavin's her real father," Sobers said. "With Forbes dead, perhaps Glavin has some legal rights."

Doris said nothing. Peter Cole seemed to go stiff. His boyish face was suddenly sweating.

"There . . . there's a cabin. Near San Vicente, Mrs. Forbes, you remember? It's abandoned up a canyon. I guess you all sort of forgot about it, but Gloria and I fixed it up, used to go out there. I wonder if maybe she and Glavin—?"

"The old ranch!" Doris cried. "Of course! Paul, if she's out there . . . ! We have to tell the police!"

"Call Hoag or Beckett," Sobers said.

She hurried into the study. Sobers faced Peter Cole.

"You just happened to remember that cabin now?"

"Yes, I'm sorry."

"No," Sobers said. "You know she's there, don't you."

Peter sat down. "I . . . drove out there. I saw someone. Not Gloria, hobos maybe. They go out there. I didn't think anything of it until . . . now."

"Yeh," Sobers said. "Sure."

Doris came from the study. "Paul? I can't. I can't call Hoag. I want to be there, talk to Johnny. I'm afraid, Paul. I can talk to him, I know I can. If the police go alone, Johnny might . . . he might . . ."

"All right," Sobers said. "Let's go."

*

The Sussex is the best restaurant in San Vicente. Roy Butler liked that. It made him feel good to eat in the hushed glitter among the affluent and powerful, to watch them look at him, wonder who he was, sure he was someone.

He *was* someone—the handsomest man in the room, in a three-hundred-dollar suit, drinking brandy with his coffee, and taking the wrapper off a dark $2.50 cigar. Aware of the tall, thin woman watching him from the bar. Over thirty and skinny in a red sheath dress, but it was an expensive sheath dress, and she looked at him instead of at the man with her.

A waiter bent close. "Mr. Butler? Telephone."

He took it in the foyer. "Yeh, Butler . . . Where? A cabin . . . Okay, yeh."

He hung up, looked back toward where the thin woman in the red dress still sat at the bar. Then he went out to his car, took a pistol from the glove compartment, slipped it into his suit coat pocket, and drove out of the parking lot.

*

The sun was setting into twilight as Doris drove the red Mercedes through Monteverde and turned west to-

184

ward the coast. Sobers sat beside her in the front seat, half turned to face her.

"Sandra Innes talked to Butler a few months ago," he said. "She talked to someone else, too, and had a call from L.A. about when Forbes was out of town that night. She was being paid by someone—for eighteen years. Now she's dead."

Doris drove. "I'm sorry. I never liked her, but I'm sorry."

"She'd put a lot of time into Walter Unger back then. She figured she was owed something when he got killed."

Doris said nothing, her eyes on the twilight road.

"You had a bad marriage, so you found another man," Sobers said. "Glavin caught you, killed the man. Forbes prosecuted Glavin. Later you married Forbes. Sad, but how bad really? Husbands and wives do grow apart, fall in love with other people. Forbes had to prosecute—it was his job, and he made a fair deal. Is it really enough for revenge eighteen years later by a man who has a new life doing what he always wanted to do?"

Her voice was flat. "Isn't it?"

"When I talked to Glavin, he said, 'Jesus God, what they did!' Forbes lived with guilt. Josh Brady says that Walter Unger wasn't your type of man."

"Brady? He always hated me!"

"Walter Unger *wasn't* your type, Doris." Sobers watched her beautiful profile in the fading twilight, the smell of the sea close now. "But he was a man who would never refuse a woman if she hinted he could have her. You gave him that hint, met him that once only, and arranged for Glavin to catch you. You wanted him in trouble so you could have your real lover, Henry Forbes. You and Forbes were lovers long before Johnny killed Unger."

Her face was immobile, almost invisible.

"You set him up," Sobers said. "Somehow, in the years since, he realized the truth. Guessed or found out."

She was crying. Silent tears that streamed down.

"I better drive," Sobers said. "Pull over, and—"

"No." Her voice was steady even as she cried. "Our marriage was killing me. I met Henry, but Johnny would never let me go, and there was Gloria. It was adultery—divorce was harder then and his father had lawyers. I could have lost Gloria! Unger wanted me, I went to him. We let Johnny find out. He was drunk, he'd be violent. We'd prove that nothing really happened between me and Unger, just friends, and everyone would think that Johnny was unstable and dangerous, and I could divorce him without losing Gloria. But Johnny *killed* Unger! That wasn't supposed to happen! Murder, and we'd set it up!"

Her small hands were white on the steering wheel. "Unger was dead. Everyone knew he was a lecher. No one would doubt that we were having a real affair except—"

"Sandra Innes. She knew Unger wasn't in an affair with you. So you paid her to lie, and you've been paying her ever since."

The sea was dark and silver to the right now.

"All I wanted . . ." She became silent for a time. "Now you know why I can't hurt Johnny. He has the right to want us dead!"

"No one has that right, Doris. One crime doesn't justify another, that's our code. We don't have the right of revenge, of vendetta. You should have told all this from the start."

"I . . . I couldn't."

They had passed the exits to Fremont, were coming close to the outskirts of San Vicente.

186

"Turn off at the airport," Sobers said. "There's no way of knowing where revenge will lead, where it will stop, who it will involve. Does Roy Butler know the truth, Doris? Is he blackmailing you, too? Money to keep him from telling Gloria?"

"Roy? No, Paul, he's not doing anything like that!"

"All right. My car's at the airport. Drop me, and go for the sheriff. I'll drive to the cabin. We've lost enough time."

When she had gone, Sobers took back roads following her directions and turned into the narrow mountain canyon. At a sharp curve in the dirt road, he saw the light of a cabin ahead through the twisted oaks. He pulled off the road and worked cautiously toward the cabin through the thick mesquite and the trees. It stood on a small rise, a porch in front and light in its bare windows. Sobers saw no one moving . . . and then he did.

Not in the house or on the porch, but near the porch.

In the brush moving close, and then up over the railing and onto the porch. Crouched there a moment, silent.

A man with a gun in his hand.

Who stood and stepped quickly into the cabin through the open door, his face clear for an instant in the light of the doorway.

Roy Butler.

22

No sounds came from the cabin. Sobers crawled through the thorny brush of the canyon, the sticky sap of the wild sage gumming his hands. A Chevelle station wagon was parked on the road side of the cabin. On the mountain side, the lighted window was low against the slope. Sobers reached it and raised up.

Roy Butler stood in the center of the room, his gun in his hand. On a narrow cot, John Glavin sat with his back against the wall, his hands in the pockets of his worn jeans, and his thick legs crossed lazily at the ankles. He lounged casually, but his small eyes were fixed toward Butler, sharp and bright.

Gloria stood almost between them.

"I said go on out of here!" Roy Butler said to her.

"I won't!" She was afraid. "For God's sake, Roy, he's my father!"

Butler slashed the air with the gun. "He's a killer you never met before in your life."

"Please?" Tears in her eyes. "Put the gun down."

On the cot Glavin leaned. Butler swung the gun. The

big poet's eyes glittered, but he sat back again.

"He's dangerous," Butler said. "He wants to kill me, and he'll kill you, too!"

The handsome schemer's voice cracked, almost a squeak. Out in the night a laugh rose in Sobers' throat. But he didn't laugh. Butler wasn't funny now, not in that cabin. As nervous and jumpy as a schoolboy watching his first woman unbutton her blouse, but not funny.

"No," Gloria said.

"No," John Glavin said. "Put the gun—"

"He killed Forbes and damn knows who else, but he's not going to get me! Get out, Gloria. Now!"

Glavin said, "Self-defense? He's going to shoot me in self-defense, kid."

"I won't go with you, Roy! I won't let you—"

"Outside!" Butler said, almost croaked.

"Roy?" Gloria said. "I'll marry you. All right? I—"

"Marry?" Butler laughed. "Thanks for nothing."

On the cot Glavin leaned forward again. "This isn't his idea, an errand boy. Someone else's dirty work. What's in it for you, errand boy?"

"Shut up!"

Butler's handsome face sweated, and he talked too much. Sobers saw it—Butler was scared to death. Talk was his world, not guns, and he was scared. John Glavin had seen it, too, and slowly sat back once more, his eyes wary and nervous. A scared man with a gun in his hand is dangerous—like a time bomb.

"My car's up the road," Butler said to Gloria.

Sobers dropped down and crawled to where the shadowy porch rose above him in the moonlight. He climbed up quietly. He was halfway up when the moonlight was suddenly blotted out. A shape that loomed up between Sobers and the moon.

189

Someone was on the porch.

Something hit him hard and high on the head.

*

Nowhere is ever totally silent. The night canyon and the lighted cabin above him were as close to it as Sobers had ever heard.

He lay in the brush and listened to the silence. Not even distant traffic sounds. Nothing. An empty canyon, and sometimes it was hard to realize that there were still empty canyons. A total silence, as if the night itself were hiding from some monster, holding its breath.

Sobers sat up. His head spun. He held to a bush until he steadied. Then he raised his hand gently to feel the side of his head. It was tender just above the bandage, and the whole bandage was damp. The wound was bleeding. Not much, but enough to make him feel weak as he stood up slowly.

He was still in the shadow of the cabin porch in the moonlight. The moon had hardly moved in the black sky. On the ground no more than fifteen minutes and unconscious less than a quarter of that. Semiconscious, shocked by the opening of his head wound, but with vague dreams of a floating scream, feet fast on wood, a car engine, shots . . . Shots?

The silence seemed to brood as if the night were bent in sorrow, contemplating some dark question. He climbed to the porch, looked in at the open front door where the light streamed out into the silence.

Roy Butler lay on his back like a rag doll, limp legs sprawled, mouth open, dead eyes staring up.

Sobers bent over the incredible face that would never grow ugly. The body was warm, even hot. The two holes in his chest were close together, there wasn't much blood. His gun lay only inches from his hand. Sobers sniffed. It hadn't been fired.

190

He touched nothing—that was for the police—and stood up. He lit a cigarette as he looked down at the dead man. A hollow man who had drifted from day to shapeless day while everything he wanted seemed to slip through his grasping fingers. Shot twice from in front while he had a pistol in his hand, and the pistol unfired. The shapeless will, the indecision that had made everything elude him, had finally cost him his life. A born loser in a world where only winning counted.

Lee Beckett was behind him. "Butler?"

"Yes," Sobers said. "He came for Gloria."

As deputies spread quickly through the cabin, Sobers told Beckett what had happened. Sheriff Hoag strode in, stopped.

"You finally did it, Sobers."

"Damn it, Hoag, shut up!" Beckett was angry. "Sobers hasn't shot anyone. This is all long past Sobers."

"He's a fugitive! He attacked Ruston with a—"

"For God's sake, drop that, too. He's a stubborn idiot stumbling around after who killed his wife. We haven't helped him much. You think he shot Butler? Find the gun."

Beckett crouched over the body. Hoag motioned for a deputy to search Sobers. The deputy patted Sobers expertly, shook his head. Angrily Hoag ordered a search for the murder gun.

Doris Forbes stood in the doorway. "What . . . ? Paul?"

"Roy Butler," Sobers said. He told her the story.

"They . . . they took Gloria with them?"

"It looks like it," Sobers said.

Lee Beckett stood up. "Looks like a .32-caliber again, same as Gloria and Sandra Innes. Keys in his pockets, matches from the Sussex Restaurant, cigarettes, a wallet with no credit cards. I guess he wasn't a good risk, the credit people know what they're doing. But there's two hundred in cash in the wallet, and his clothes are all brand new."

A deputy came to Hoag. "No gun in the cabin or outside."

Hoag said, "Look harder."

"Where was he getting money?" Sobers said to Beckett and Doris.

"I . . . I don't know, Paul," Doris said.

Beckett walked out of the cabin and down off the porch to where the station wagon had been parked. There was torn brush where the car had slewed and yawed off the driveway.

"They left in a hurry," Beckett said. "Probably beat us to the mouth of the canyon. Could be north, south, east, or west by now." He half swore and half sighed. "We'll get out the call and then wait." He looked up as Sheriff Hoag joined them. "Find the gun?"

"No," Hoag said. "I suppose Sobers—"

"Sheriff!"

A deputy stood where the driveway from the cabin joined the canyon road. Twin tracks in the thick brush showed where a car had cut too sharply from the driveway to the road—a car turned not toward the canyon exit but deeper into the mountains.

"Get Mrs. Forbes back to town," Beckett said to a deputy.

"No!" Doris cried. "I'm coming with you! I can talk to Johnny. I want—"

"I don't give a damn what you want now, Mrs. Forbes," Beckett said. "There won't be much talking now. Take her."

The deputy looked at Sheriff Hoag. Hoag nodded, but he wasn't happy. The deputy took Doris.

"What's up that way?" Sobers asked.

"A couple of shacks," Beckett said, "and a way out, up top to Camino Cielo—the sky road. The canyon road's a goat track up high, hard even for a good four-wheel drive. I don't think an ordinary wagon can make it. Come on."

Beckett, with Sobers beside him, drove out first.

*

The twisting canyon road had just begun to climb sharply in tortured switchbacks when they heard the shots.

Two shots that reverberated through the narrow canyon in the moonlit night.

"Up there!" Sobers said.

He pointed ahead and to the right where an almost invisible track led off into the brush and twisted trees. No more than twin ruts in the hard adobe soil, it vanished into the oaks like a darker tunnel in the night.

"There's a shack up there," Beckett said.

The column of police cars stopped on the narrow road, and the deputies fanned out in the night, forming a line that moved up the mountain slope through the trees toward the shack above.

Two more shots exploded ahead in the darkness.

They echoed and re-echoed off the steep canyon walls, and rising over the echoes there came a long, anguished howl—a howl of rage and frustration ahead and above, like the last despairing cry of some trapped animal.

"Good God, what—?" Sheriff Hoag said hoarsely.

A savage, chilling cry of hate that hung in the dark canyon, and as the line of deputies moved up the slope their eyes searched the night uneasily. High up through the trees the faint, half-hidden outline of an unpainted shack took shape.

"Beckett!" Sobers whispered.

"Watch it!" Hoag said.

They had both seen the movement above on the dark slope.

"Watch out for the girl!" Beckett said along the line of deputies.

Two shapes seemed to flit among the shadowy trees between the distant, half-seen shack and the waiting line of deputies below. Silvery shapes in the patches of moonlight, moving erratically down the mountainside like floating ghosts.

Or only one shape, plunging and crashing down and down in desperate escape or wild charge.

"Ready!" Hoag shouted.

A single figure closer now, stumbling and falling and staggering up again to plunge on in a weaving path.

"It's Gloria!" Sobers cried.

"Hold fire!" Beckett yelled.

The figure became a girl as Gloria Forbes slipped and slid and stumbled down through the line of deputies to collapse on the dark ground behind them. Beckett, Hoag, and Sobers hurried to her. She lay breathing hard, her clothes torn and her hair tangled with brush. Sobers and Beckett helped her to sit up. Her eyes were dark holes in her gaunt face.

"He's gone wild up there. Jack Tracy. Manic!" She looked at them all as if she were sure they knew exactly what she was talking about. "He's insane. For a long time, I suppose. Now his mind's all gone. We could see that. He doesn't know where he is, even who he is. After he shot Roy, he made us drive up here. My father told him the wagon couldn't make it out this way. He wouldn't listen, not even to my father. Then he saw the road going up and told my father to drive up there to that shack. We heard you coming, all the cars, and that's when he went manic, Tracy did. He had his gun, turned on me. My father stopped him, got me away. He knocked Tracy down, got me out. We ran. We saw you down here and we ran. We could hear Tracy howl behind us, but my father made me just keep running. We—"

She stopped. She looked all around in the silvery night. The shock in her hollow eyes turned into confusion, question.

"My father? Where is he?"

Sobers said, "You came down alone, Gloria."

"No, no!" She was impatient with their stupidity. "We ran together. My father got me away. He hit Tracy, and—"

"He didn't come down, Gloria," Sheriff Hoag said.

She looked at them and then she looked back up the slope in the dark moonlight. She stood up as if she had to go back up to find out. Sobers held her arm.

"Let's go get them," Beckett said.

The line of deputies moved up the tangled slope in the moonlight. In a converging semicircle toward the shack above, they moved faster now, with Gloria safe and the rising urgency that comes when the end is in sight. Twenty yards below the shack the deputy called low.

"Over here."

John Glavin lay face down in the brush. Three deputies turned him over carefully and Beckett kneeled in the night.

"Shot twice, shoulder and back. He's breathing; there's not much blood." Beckett searched the massive poet. "No gun on him. Looks like he was hit before he left the shack up there, made it this far with Gloria."

"I never saw him with a gun," Gloria said. She sat down in the thorny brush beside the big man. She brushed the hair from his closed eyes, began to softly stroke his thick hair. She whispered low to him in the darkness.

195

Then she sat bathed in a blaze of light.

"What—!" Hoag cried.

Headlights glared beside the shack above. Swinging twin shafts of hard light, the station wagon already moving down the steep, rutted track from the shack to the road below, its engine roaring full.

"He's going down!"

The station wagon hurtled past the last man in the line, careening down the slope, tearing up brush, sideswiping trees, trying to stay in the ruts but going too fast already and making a road where there was none.

"Get him!" Hoag yelled.

The line of deputies turned and ran back down the slope.

"No way," Beckett said, "he's doing fifty!"

Sobers stopped running. The whole line stopped. They stood there in the dark watching the red taillights hurl down to the road below, the twin shafts of the headlights probe the trees and the road and the far side of the canyon. It was Sobers who said it:

"He's got no legs. He can't drive."

The station wagon reached the canyon road. By then it was doing sixty. It seemed to try to turn into the road, tilted for an instant on two wheels, hung, and then fell back onto all four wheels. It plunged straight on across the canyon road into the brush, sheared off two large oaks, and smashed head-on into a great boulder set into the far side of the canyon.

The rear end rose high to flip over, hung suspended, and dropped back in a silvery cloud of dust.

There was no fire, and the dust was still settling when Beckett, Sobers, and the deputies reached it. The front end was crushed back to the windshield. Jack Tracy sat with the steering column protruding from his back. His

thick elephant shoes were rigid under the crushed dash-
board, nowhere near the brakes.

The small .32-caliber pistol was on the seat beside
the dead pencil seller.

23

Outside the high windows of the hospital dawn came clear over San Vicente. Doris Forbes and Gloria sat on a couch in the waiting room. Sobers stood against the wall near them. Lee Beckett dozed in a chair until a doctor strode in.

"Glavin's out of surgery," the doctor reported. "The sheriff has the bullets. He's in recovery, we'll put him in I.C.U. in an hour or so. It'll be touch and go for some time."

"I'll have a guard at I.C.U.," Beckett said.

An hour later, Sheriff Hoag came into the waiting room. His bland face was solemn, but his eyes were almost smiling. Beckett told him the doctor's report.

"We'll get Glavin's story, but we have most of it anyway," Hoag said. He sat down. "The gun Jack Tracy had in the car shot them all: Roy Butler, Gloria, Sandra Innes and Glavin. We know that one of them shot Henry Forbes and Susan Sobers with Forbes's own gun, so that wraps it up."

Hoag sat back, satisfaction in his voice, "Glavin faked

dying in Wyoming to set up his revenge. But Roy Butler wanted to marry Gloria, knew he had to split her from her parents, so dug into the past. Glavin knew that if Butler dug up too much the truth would come out and ruin his revenge cover-up. So he and Tracy came out here to stop Butler, or to act before his cover was blown, or both. They found out that Sandra Innes had talked to Butler so paid her to keep quiet, and Glavin moved in near Gloria to watch. He used Kapek's name because he still had Kapek's papers. He shot Susan Sobers but missed Roy Butler at Ruston's clinic, and then Butler ran off with Gloria. Tracy followed them, while Glavin kept close to Forbes."

Sobers said, "Tracy couldn't drive. How did he follow Gloria and Butler? The killer up in Marin had a car."

"He got a driver," Hoag said. "Tracy was easy to re-member, it didn't take us an hour to find the driver. Pancho Guerro—that's one of his names, anyway. He'd sell his mother for a nickel, and he was in Soledad with Tracy and Glavin. He drove Tracy around this week, too. He's talking nicely, admits he took Tracy to Marin and saw the shooting up there.

"I guess Tracy thought he'd killed Roy Butler, and Glavin went ahead and killed Forbes. He made it look like suicide, but Mrs. Forbes said it wasn't, Sobers was bumbling around, and Roy Butler turned up alive! They really wanted to silence Butler then, but they couldn't find him."

"Tracy tried," Sobers said. "I guess he tried to stop me, too. Tipped Dr. Ruston I was coming to see him with a gun."

"That he did," Hoag said. "Then they got a break—when we found Gloria it looked like Forbes had shot her and himself. They were clear. Butler seemed too scared to talk, so they went home. Or Glavin did. Maybe it was only Forbes he hated all along. But Gloria and Sobers didn't let it rest."

"Lucky for us," Beckett said. "We did our best for Glavin."

"Mistakes are made," Hoag said stiffly. "Tracy tried to hide the trail by killing Sandra Innes, and they tried to stop Sobers when he showed up in New York. But they bungled it, and when Gloria appeared on their doorstep they became desperate and came back here to try to cover up the whole affair. They had Gloria. If they could silence Roy Butler, Sobers, and Mrs. Forbes, they might get away. Except Sobers and Butler found them first. Tracy knocked Sobers out and killed Butler at the cabin. They would probably have killed Sobers and Gloria then, too, but they heard us coming so left Sobers and ran with Gloria."

"My father saved me from Tracy!" Gloria cried.

"Did he?" Hoag said. "If he really wanted to protect you, why did he wait until the last minute?"

Gloria looked at the floor, said nothing.

"I'll tell you why," Hoag said. "He knew by then that we had them trapped. Saving you would make him look good. He could blame it all on Tracy—his pal who'd gone crazy. Neat."

"She's his daughter," Doris said. "He had to save her."

"Maybe," Hoag snapped, "but he'd let Tracy do his dirty work all along. Except that he just had to kill Henry Forbes himself, and that'll hang him. I expect he planned to make it look like suicide from the start. That's why he stole Forbes's gun, and had it when he shot Susan Sobers. He had to have taken the gun from the Forbes house, and who else knew the house so well, eh? It had been his house once, he knew it like a book."

200

"Glavin shot my wife trying to kill Butler?" Sobers said.

"Or maybe he wanted them both dead," Hoag said. "Your wife was too close to Butler, might know too much. He'll tell us."

"We don't have much if he doesn't," Beckett said.

"We've got the motive, it'll do fine," Hoag said.

A doctor appeared. "You can see him now if you want. He's stable for now, but I doubt if he can talk much."

"Will he . . . Will he live?" Doris asked.

"We don't know yet."

The guard at I.C.U. opened the door for them. John Glavin lay in a corner bed behind a curtain like some great monolith. His massive arms were crossed on his slowly rising and falling chest, and his beard lay above the sheet.

"You recognize him, Mrs. Forbes?" Beckett asked.

"I . . . It's been a long time," she said.

She moved closer. Glavin suddenly shifted in the bed, and his small eyes flickered open. He stared up at Doris. His eyes widened. Slowly, he nodded. His hand moved.

Doris recoiled. Then she stopped. She smiled.

"Johnny?" she said.

Glavin stared up. For a second he seemed almost to smile. Then his eyes closed, and he lay back motionless. A nurse came up. She examined him quickly.

"He's sleeping. You all better go now."

"I'll stay," Gloria said. "He's my father."

*

Sobers stood in the hospital parking lot. On a hill, the hospital had a sweeping view of the channel islands sharp and clear far out over the sea. Sobers didn't look at the view. He looked back at the hospital where John Glavin lay alone and silent.

201

He returned to the lobby, looked up Lois Butler's home telephone, and dialed. There was no answer. He went out to his car and drove across the city through the early morning streets. At her office building he saw her car alone in the parking area.

On the upper gallery her door was unlocked. The outer office was empty. He went into the inner office. She sat behind her desk, a bottle and a glass on the desk. She looked haggard.

"I thought that perhaps work . . ." She shrugged.

"Why is Roy dead, Lois? What really killed him?"

She poured whisky, looked at it. "I've made an odd discovery. Women with careers make the same mistakes men with careers do, the same stupid actions. Maybe it's not sex or psychology that determines, but only work. We are what we do."

"Why was he digging up the past? For Gloria, yes, but not for love. Not Roy."

"Will I end up like any other old, single lawyer? Rich, going bald, buying young law clerks for my fun?"

"He had money, new clothes, a better deal than Gloria."

"Even the bottle in the office desk for comfort," she said. "Because my brother is dead, and my man hates me now."

"Some money scheme," Sobers said. "That's what killed Roy."

She drank. "I killed him."

"How?"

She touched the bottle with a single finger as if wondering what it was. "In bed one night, a little drunk, Russ told me he had pulled a coup that would put Newmont on the map. An enormous gift from Otto Genseric —land, buildings, money. A monument for Genseric, status for Newmont, and fame for Dr. Russell Taylor."

202

She refilled her glass. "A few months ago Roy was played out, desperate. So I told him about Russ's big deal. Land had to be involved, subcontracts, options, commissions, and there's always money to be picked up. I didn't know details or what land was involved, but Roy could handle that."

"You know what land was involved now, don't you?"

She nodded. "The same mistakes, men and women. The same stupidities, the same zeroes in the end. All Roy's schemes zero in the end." She drank. "I'll be fine, maybe even a judge."

Sobers walked out.

*

Otto Genseric lived ten miles south of San Vicente in the next county. A community called Dorinda Isle. Sobers found it on a large bay a mile off the freeway.

A U-shaped artificial island that looked like a walled castle complete with moat. There was no drawbridge, just an ordinary bridge with a barricade and guard house. The guard took his name and business, made a call, and raised the barricade.

"Left over the bridge, ninth house on the right."

On both sides of the single road the houses were individually walled, the front yards a few square feet of grass around driveways into the garages. But these houses went for up to a million dollars without the owners batting an eye, and the real front yards were in the back around patios and docks. A big houseman opened Otto Genseric's gate, took Sobers around to the front.

Genseric sat on the deck of a large motor cruiser. The vigorous old man was out of his boots for once, in a bathing suit and short robe, but he still wore the gray Stetson.

"What do you want, Mr. Sobers?"

"I hear you plan a large gift to Newmont College."

203

"That is my private affair."

"The police in San Vicente have a lot of shot and dead people," Sobers said, "and I don't think they really know why yet. One of the dead is my wife, and when they kill your wife, you want to know why. I want to know very badly. That could make me awfully irresponsible; full of wild charges, crazy accusations, nasty publicity."

The old man seemed to think about that under the wide brim of his Stetson, his eyes hidden in the brim shadow.

"It's no secret," he said. "Calixco Petroleum will endow Newmont to establish a faculty of petroleum engineering. I am personally giving a chair of economic philosophy to be jointly appointed by the college and myself, a library, and a petroleum museum. The Genseric Memorial Library will eventually house my collection of business publications and my personal papers."

"How much for all that?"

"Some twenty million dollars in all, but it's my dream, and a dream is more than money. It is deductible, of course. Call it my monument. Something I will leave behind."

Sobers nodded. "Kilroy was here."

"What?"

"Nothing, a thought," Sobers said. "Why Newmont?"

"The small, independent colleges are the hope of this nation. Where the truth can be taught, not alien lies."

"Russell Taylor agrees with you," Sobers said. "Calixco's faculty of petroleum engineering, your chair of economic philosophy, your library, your ideas. Are you buying a college, Mr. Genseric?"

"I wouldn't say that," Genseric snapped.

"Not many colleges would go for it. What convinced Taylor?"

"As you said, he agrees with my views. Then, I suppose his reputation won't be hurt. He could go far, bigger colleges."

"He'd like that," Sobers said. "What land are you buying?"

"Taylor will decide that. He knows the needs."

"You don't want to know what land you'll buy?"

"I don't bother with details, Sobers."

"No questions asked, as long as you get your college?"

"You can leave now."

"One thing. How much did you allot for the land?"

"Good-bye, Sobers."

He found his own way out. He drove back across the bridge to the freeway, and turned south in the noon sun toward Los Angeles.

*

It was dark when Gloria Forbes knocked at Peter Cole's room on the first floor of the Newmont College dormitory.

"How is your father?" Peter asked as he let her in.

Gloria looked at the room with its rows of books and impersonal dormitory furniture as if she had never really seen it.

"The doctors say it's still touch and go," she said. "But he's conscious and says he's hungry. He's amazing."

"Gloria! He killed—"

"Peter?" She sat down, closed her eyes. "When I was at the cabin, someone drove close, watched, then drove off. I thought it was your car, and mother says you told her and Paul that I might be at the cabin." She looked at him. "You *knew* I was at the cabin. I'd called you."

"You told me not to tell," Peter said. "You were with your father. I didn't want to butt in. I—"

"Tracy pulled the cord," she said, her mouth thin. "The line went dead. You must have wondered, been alarmed."

"Yes," he said. His back to her, he stood looking out the dark window of the small room, looking at his image in the dark glass. "I wondered. I was alarmed. I drove out to the cabin."

She watched his back. "It *was* you? And you just drove away—"

"Sobers had told us about Glavin and Tracy, about what he thought they had done." He seemed hypnotized by his own face in the window, his voice toneless. "I drove out there. I saw them at the cabin. I was afraid. I was scared to be involved."

He remained at the window with his back to her. She sat and looked at his back for some minutes before she became aware of someone else in the room and turned her head. Sobers stood just inside the door. He closed the door, spoke to Peter.

"What else didn't you want to be involved in, Peter?"

Cole turned to look at Sobers, but he didn't speak.

"You mentioned an offer to buy the Forbes house and land," Sobers said. "No one else had ever talked about that. Doris knew, and probably others, and certainly Gloria, but no one thought it important enough to mention—except you. Why?"

Gloria frowned. "There was nothing special about it, Paul."

"Routine?" Sobers said. "Were you going to sell?"

"Well, Mother and Henry said maybe I should this time. I'll be leaving home; the beach house would do for them."

"Who made the offer?"

"Some company. M and R Investments, I think. Why, Paul?"

Sobers said, "Tell her, Peter. About Otto Genseric's gift to Newmont. A museum and a library. On what land, Peter?"

Cole's voice was dull. "Where everyone would see them. A cliff overlooking the whole campus. The Forbes land."

"Rezoned, of course," Sobers said. "M and R buys the land for two hundred fifty thousand dollars, Genseric gets it rezoned and buys it for a million! Legal, if smelly, and odors get easily overlooked these days—unless Gloria got wind of it herself and held out for the full million. She'd get it. Genseric really wants that land. And that's where Roy Butler came in.

"He knew about the deal. If he married Gloria, he'd tell her, and they could grab the whole million. If Gloria, later, didn't like why he'd married her, I suppose he figured he could manage to get his hands on a lot of it before she dumped him. So that's why he went digging around in the past."

Gloria stood up. "Peter?"

"I'm sorry, Gloria." He sat on his cot. "I . . . I—"

"He knew," Sobers said, "but he wasn't part of it."

"Who was, Paul?"

"Let's take a ride," Sobers said.

She turned to Cole, who sat with his face in his hands. "Peter?" she said. "Good-bye."

Peter Cole nodded. When they left, he was crying—not for Gloria, for himself.

24

In the Intensive Care Unit, Lee Beckett stood outside the curtain around John Glavin's bed while a nurse worked on the poet. Beckett carried a small black case.

"Are you thinking the same thing I am?" Sobers said. "Would a man who wanted everyone to think he was dead so he could kill an enemy really act so stupid? Live openly under his real name, publish a book? It doesn't make much sense, does it?"

"What does make sense?" Beckett asked.

The nurse came out. "You can go in. He's alert."

John Glavin lay on his back, surrounded by machines and full of tubes. Behind the hair, his eyes glinted at them.

Sobers stood over the big man. "Why pretend to die, then go on using the dead name no matter how far away from people who knew you? Why wait over ten years for revenge? No, I don't think you wanted revenge, and if John Glavin didn't want revenge, he'd have no reason to hide the past. Tracy would have had no reason to do what he did. But you're not John Glavin."

Gloria said, "Paul, no! He's my—"

"He's not your father. That's what he wanted hidden."

Beckett touched the case he carried. "I've got a set of John Glavin's fingerprints and a printing kit."

"Johnny died," the big man said. "Strike three. Okay."

"Glavin and the drifter Ward died," Sobers said. "It was Frank Kapek who lived, and Kapek's fingerprints that were substituted for Ward's. You—Frank Kapek— lived, and then took John Glavin's name, wrote John Glavin's poems."

"Why?" Beckett said. "Frank Kapek isn't wanted anywhere."

"Other people want a guy besides cops," Frank Kapek said. "Some things you keep going. You wouldn't understand."

"Try us," Beckett said.

Frank Kapek lay breathing carefully. "Johnny, he died first. Not strong, didn't care. Like that in the joint, too. Me and Jack took him over inside, helped, figured out what that wife had done to him. Johnny didn't even remember hitting that Unger. Never heard about Unger before that night. The wife had a guy, but Unger wasn't right. We wised Johnny up. When we got out, Sandra Innes told us. Didn't matter. Johnny didn't care no more."

His eyes watched the ceiling as if seeing beyond it. "There was no one in the joint like Johnny. A poet. Me and Jack got him through. Since I was a kid I wrote poems. Johnny, he showed me how. Didn't write much himself, helped me. We all helped each other. Outside, in Wyoming, Johnny got better. He started writing again."

His bearded face turned. "The blizzard hit. Johnny went first. Ward next. Jack's legs froze. Three days me and Jack waited. I wrote a big poem. To Johnny. Jack said it sounded like Johnny. Maybe we were delirious. I felt like Johnny. Jack said I *was* Johnny. When they found us, we decided. Johnny had a talent, a vision. The blizzard was a sign. A second chance. For Johnny, for me. You wouldn't understand."

"Go on," Gloria said. "Please! Go on."

Kapek looked toward her from the sterile bed. "Johnny, he'd lost his vision and his voice. We'd give it back to him. I'd be his voice. Finish his work. Be what he'd wanted to be. A second chance—for Johnny and for me. I was a punk, a crook, a drunk. With punk friends and punk enemies. Inside, with Johnny, I'd changed. Outside I was sliding right back. The old ways, the old friends, the old enemies. They'd never leave me alone. I wouldn't want to be left alone. But John Glavin? He had no punk enemies. He had pride, talent. He could make it. And he did. I am a poet. Good or bad."

"A joining," Gloria said. "Two people who became a third."

"Maybe only something to work for," Sobers said.

Beckett said, "Or an impersonation and a cover."

"Okay, maybe just a cover," Frank Kapek said. His voice was stronger. "Johnny had a name. Frank Kapek had enemies. It'll do if you want, and it worked. Ten years I've been straight, and my poems are published. John Glavin's a pretty good poet now, and Frank Kapek's out of the joint. Or he was, then that Roy Butler came snooping around."

"You were afraid of being exposed?" Beckett said.

"I didn't like it, but it was Jack mostly. It was all a second chance for Jack, too. I make enough writing, lecturing, teaching private classes to keep us both going. Jack was an editor now, not a pencil seller anymore. He was scared that if the past came out I'd give it up, blow it. He was right. When Butler showed, I quit working, started drinking, fell apart. Frank Kapek, punk! For a couple of months. I guess Jack just didn't want to lose what he had."

He moved, pulling at the tubes in him. "Maybe he was half crazy since he lost the legs. I didn't know, maybe I didn't want to know. He came out here with his pencils. I followed. He said he was watching Butler. I never knew what he was really doing until Sobers came to New York. I helped Sobers, but I couldn't blow the whistle. Jack was my buddy. In the joint that means something. You don't turn up your buddy.

"Gloria showed up, Jack took her here, I came after. I kept Gloria near where I could protect her, held Jack back from doing anything. Then Butler had to pull his gun, and Jack flipped all the way. He wasn't Jack anymore."

"So he didn't want to lose your money," Beckett said. "His free ride, maybe big prospects for the future."

"If that's easier for you," Kapek said. "Only what he really wanted was to be someone. His name in poet John Glavin's bio. A footnote, but something to say that Jack Tracy was here."

Gloria put her hand gently on his thick arm.

"Sorry, kid," he said.

"He was dead all my life," she said. "You gave him back to me. In a way, you really are him."

Sobers said, "You, or Tracy, had no reason to kill Forbes, did you? He wanted the past buried as much as you. Can you go on being John Glavin alone? The poet, a voice."

Kapek was silent. "Maybe. I can try."

"Beckett?" Sobers said. "Who has to know? Tracy's dead."

Beckett nodded. "He should have turned Tracy in earlier, but I think I can swing it."

*

Russell Taylor stood to meet Sobers and Gloria when they came into his book-lined library. He wasn't alone. Dr. Martin Ruston sat behind him with a highball.

"Your father," Taylor said to Gloria, "is he—?"

Sobers said, "We know what Roy Butler was doing."

"What?" Taylor blinked. "Butler?"

"Peter told us. I talked to Genseric and Lois. Genseric'll say he was duped now. He didn't call to warn you, did he?"

Dr. Ruston put down his highball. Taylor smiled at Sobers and Gloria. He stopped smiling.

"The stupid, stupid bastards! They didn't have to—"

"Them?" Dr. Ruston said. "You! Your stupid talking!"

Sobers nodded, "Yes, you had to be part of it, Ruston. The M and R Investments team. And when Gloria wouldn't play ball with Butler, he went to you. He knew a lot too much, so you had to cut him in on the scheme."

"Sobers?" Russell Taylor said. "Butler's dead, you know? His share could become your—"

"A twenty million dollar prize for Newmont, a master stroke for you," Sobers said, "but you just had to grab for that extra rake-off. I'll bet you felt real clever."

Ruston said, "You'll never amount to a thing, Sobers."

"Paul?" Gloria said. "I don't understand why Genseric let them do it? Why not buy from me and save all that money?"

"Because he wants his monument, his library, and Taylor has to okay the deal. It's all a tax write-off anyway. A bribe gets no write-off and could cause trouble, so the little deal was fine. If it misfired, Genseric could claim he knew nothing about it."

"All right," Dr. Ruston said, "you've exposed us. But

212

since it won't happen now, we've done nothing! We're not responsible for Roy Butler. So if that's all, you can get out of here."

"Not quite all," Sobers said. "Butler caused one more thing. He knew the deal. He was chasing Gloria, nosing all around the Forbeses. There was one person who would stop it all before it got started if he had even a hint of it. A lawyer, a man—"

"Henry!" Gloria cried.

Sobers nodded. "When Butler started talking to you, they had to get Henry Forbes out of the way. That's one more item Butler had found out. He had an address: *Stein Pavilion, Griffith Memorial Hospital, L.A.* I went down there today."

"Sobe—!" Ruston snapped. "I warn v   tor—"

"We   ten s and mac   ers said.

car   reoc-

"Of course," Sobers said, "once he got east they'd have taken new X-rays. That was no sweat. Ruston would have been shocked, a terrible error, the fault of some technician or clerk. He would have insisted they be very sure back east, keep Forbes for a complete study. But Forbes didn't go east. He was full of guilt, the past was coming up thanks to Roy Butler, cancer was the last straw. He shot himself. The police were right."

Taylor's voice was choked, "We never intended—"

"No, you were only greedy," Sobers said. "The kicker is I don't think they can get you for a damn thing. Not for the scheme, not for Forbes's death. Gloria might be able to sue Ruston, ruin him, but you'll both be ruined anyway when it all comes out—and I promise you it'll all come out!"

Martin Ruston took the pistol from his pocket awkwardly. He stepped toward Sobers and Gloria stiff-legged and mechanical, the gun held out in both hands. Beckett was in the doorway.

"Ruston!"

The well-tailored physician seemed to freeze.

"Ruston?" Sobers said. "You forgot to release the safety anyway."

Ruston let the gun drop. Russell Taylor sat down.

"Beckett?" Sobers said. "Can you call that assault? Maybe attempted murder? Something?"

"We can try," Beckett said. He picked up the pistol.

"Some charge for a trial," Sobers said. "Of course, my wife was an X-ray technician at the clinic. She must have spotted the faked X-rays—or just known that Henry Forbes didn't have cancer. That's why she was killed."

*

It was after midnight in the old Forbes house when Sobers finished telling it all to Doris. She made herself a martini. Sobers had a beer. Gloria had nothing.

"They told us, Mother," Gloria said.

"They would," Doris said.

"They couldn't have done it without you," Sobers said. "You controlled the land, had to convince Gloria and Henry to sell."

"To cheat me, Mother?" Gloria said. "For money?"

"I wouldn't call it that. You would get a normal price."

"What would you call it?" Sobers said.

"Opportunity! You take care of yourself."

"What was telling Henry he had cancer?"

"We had to get him away!" She seemed to consider the

214

problem again. "Genseric could have sent him away, but he never did that, and Henry would have wondered. Speed was essential. Henry often had indigestion, so it seemed . . . We never thought—"

"So you had to call it murder because you knew it was suicide and why," Sobers said. "You don't give up. You called Ruston or Taylor from Peter Cole's house and had them send Roy Butler out to that cabin to kill Glavin. With luck they might have killed each other, everything covered over. You were still trying to get what you wanted when you 'recognized' John Glavin at the hospital. You knew he wasn't really Glavin, but if you said he was, and he died, that would close the whole case."

Doris sighed. "I'm sorry about Henry. But he was weak, useless. I wanted that money. I'm sorry about your wife. They—"

"They didn't kill Susan," Sobers said. "Real killing isn't in Taylor or Ruston. Schemes and deals, not guns."

"Paul!" Gloria stared at him. "You—"

"Cancer alone didn't make Forbes kill himself," Sobers said. "Cancer—and the past. The call Sandra Innes got was from him, worried about the truth coming out, and tonight Kapek said that Glavin didn't remember hitting Unger—because he didn't hit Unger."

He looked at Doris. "A divorce from Glavin wasn't enough for you back then, you wanted his inheritance. For that Glavin had to go to prison, even to the gas chamber. Unger had to be killed. But Glavin was too drunk that night—so Forbes and you killed Unger yourselves! That was the guilt that destroyed Henry Forbes."

Doris stood calm. "You have no proof of that whatever."

"No," Sobers said, "and I don't have proof of my wife's murder. But you killed eighteen years ago, and you killed Susan."

"Did I really?"

"Only you had real access to Henry's gun and could get it back to him easily. I suppose that Susan had taken some X-rays of Forbes that showed no cancer and recognized the fakes. She wanted her share, didn't she? Tried to blackmail you."

Gloria's voice was thick, "Mother, you . . . you—"

"That bitch!" Her fine-boned face was outraged. "Trying to blackmail me! The wonderful wife Paul turned everything upside down for! As greedy as the rest of us!"

There were tears in Gloria's eyes. Doris looked at her. "She got what she deserved, Gloria!"

"I wonder if you will?" Sobers said. "Beckett?"

Beckett came in from the hall. "I got it. You better come with me, Mrs. Forbes."

In the quiet living room of the big old house, Doris Forbes looked from one of them to the other. She slowly finished her martini, set the glass down softly.

"I'll deny it, you know."

"You can do it downtown," Beckett said.

Doris nodded. She went out to the hall closet, and took out a long mink coat. She drew it close around her. For a moment her slender hands felt the rich fur with pure enjoyment.

"I'll be back soon, dear," she said to Gloria and faced Sobers. "You had to come here. Bad luck for me."

"Not for me," Gloria said.

"Ah?" Doris watched her daughter. "Have I lost that way, too? My own daughter? I hope he told you about us, Gloria. Mother *and* daughter?"

"Good-bye, Mother," Gloria said.

Doris nodded, and looked past Gloria at her image in the dark window. Then she went to Beckett, took his arm, and smiled up at him.

"Will this take very long, Mr. . . . Is it Lee?"

216

Still smiling and holding to Beckett's arm, Doris Forbes went out. Gloria sat down. Her face was stiff.

"Paul?"

"There's the gun, the motive, her admissions. But I guess it depends on what evidence they can turn up now that they know. If Taylor, or Ruston, or anyone else knew about Susan she'll go to prison. If not, she'll probably get off."

"If she does," Gloria said, "she'll be alone. I'm going with you."

*

Paul Sobers drove out of San Vicente some days later. Beckett and Sheriff Hoag were still working on charges, but Beckett wasn't hopeful. Gloria sat in the front seat of the rented car facing Sobers.

"I called my company," he said. "I told them I wanted to go on working for them, but I was going to live in Arizona. Maroldo damned me up and down, but he said he needs my work."

"They won't make it easy for us," Gloria said.

"I'm old for you, Gloria. Not a father, I hope."

"My father is dead. I can bury him now."

And he could cry for his wife now. He knew what she had wanted, and why she had died.

He drove on out of Buena Costa County. After a time they smiled at each other. That was all. There was no hurry.